FLIGHT 122

FLIGHT 122

BARRY A. MOSIER

Pacific Press® Publishing Association
Nampa, Idaho
Oshawa, Ontario, Canada
www.pacificpress.com

Cover design by Gerald Lee Monks
Cover image by Alain Wandimoyi Kyalemaninwa
Inside design by Aaron Troia

You can obtain additional copies of this book by calling toll-free 1-800-765-6955
or by visiting www.adventistbookcenter.com.

The author assumes full responsibility for the accuracy of all facts and quotations
as cited in this book.

All Scripture references are from the King James Version of the Bible.

Library of Congress Cataloging-in-Publication Data:

Mosier, Barry.
  Flight 122 : one family's story of survival and service / Barry
Mosier.
    p. cm.
  ISBN-13: 978-0-8163-2365-4 (pbk.)
  ISBN-10: 0-8163-2365-8 (pbk.)
  1. Missionary stories. 2. Seventh-day Adventists—Missions—
Africa. 3. Mosier, Barry. I. Title. II. Title: Flight one twenty-two.
  BV2087.M63   2009
  266'.67320922—dc22
  [B]
                                                    2009024112

09 10 11 12 13 • 5 4 3 2 1

Dedication

Dedicated to four special women in my life:

My mother. Viola's quiet faith has been an example in my life. Her earnest prayers carried me through difficult teen years. Her prayers for us still ascend daily before God's throne as we serve in Africa.

My wife. Marybeth has been an encouraging and loving companion. Her selfless love and acts of kindness are a constant example to me of Christian service. She is a brave missionary wife and has been a wonderful mother for our children.

My first daughter. Laura's happy outlook on life is a constant source of joy to me. She makes such wonderful grandchildren (together with her husband, Ben), and helped me with the editing of this book.

My second daughter. April is my hero. She helped to save our lives in the airplane crash by opening a hole in the plane with her bare hands. Her high energy level keeps our lives exciting!

Acknowledgment

A special thank you to Jay and Eileen Lantry, who encouraged me and edited an early draft of my manuscript.

Contents

Chapter 1

AIRPLANE CRASH

We were relaxing in our hotel room in Goma, Democratic Republic of Congo (DRC), in Central Africa. Our oldest son, Keith, who had just graduated from college, needed help launching a new supporting ministry called Congo Frontline Missions. This was my fifth visit to the country. But on this trip, my beloved wife, Marybeth, and our two children, April, age fourteen, from Ecuador, and Andrew, age four, our lively son from Tanzania, were traveling with me. Our family had been praying for more than a year for guidance about the possibility of moving from Tanzania to DRC to join Keith, and we hoped that this visit would clearly show us God's plan for us.

The two-day trip to reach Goma had included two airplane flights, two border crossings, and a three-hour car ride—and we were tired. We'd spent the previous month preparing for this trip, cramming many supplies for the new mission station into our luggage. Now, finally, we were almost there!

"I'm hungry!" April announced.

Later we sat at a restaurant table watching Andrew play race cars with the French fries on his plate. Marybeth commented, "I can't wait to see Keith! But I'm not looking forward to being in the jungle. I've told you many times I would never move to a jungle. But, if God shows us that it is His will for us to work with Keith, I'm ready to serve Him anywhere."

Reaching for Marybeth's hand, I responded, "No wonder I love you!" Marybeth tries to do God's will—even when it is contrary to her own desires and inclinations. I admire the way she follows Jesus' example, "Not My will, but Thine be done."

Excitement woke us up early the next morning. After breakfast, we took a short walk to Lake Kivu, occupying our children while waiting for our ride to the Seventh-day Adventist Union office to collect our travel papers and plane tickets.

"Ouch! Dad, this lava rock is sharp! I don't see how people in Goma can walk barefoot," April remarked as we carefully made our way down to the lake. Once there, we dipped our feet in the water while Andrew threw stones into the lake to watch them splash.

After a while, we returned to the hotel, where we prayed again for God's protection. Then we loaded our luggage into Pastor Manyama's vehicle and headed for the Union office. The vehicle lurched slowly over the potholes and lava-covered streets of Goma.

I enjoyed meeting my old friend Pastor Manyama again. He had been the treasurer of the Tanzania Union before accepting an assignment to work in North East Congo Attached Territory (NE-CAT). He would be able to give me insights into how conditions really were in DRC. In the office, Solanje, Pastor Manyama's secretary, had all our documents in order for us, and we soon left for the airport.

When we arrived at the airport, porters fought for the chance to handle our luggage. Inside the terminal, the confusion worsened. Passengers elbowed past others on their way to the counter to check their luggage. Without the help of the porters, I could be a target for pickpockets in the crowd jostling for position at the check-in counter.

"You'd better stand over there against the wall with the children while I get us checked in," I told Marybeth. I tried to keep our luggage in sight at all times. Finally, after about half an hour, we had our boarding passes for Flight 122. The man in charge of the security check held a metal-detection wand as we approached him. When I explained that we worked for a church organization, he halfheartedly waved his wand at me before beckoning us through. There wasn't any real security.

While waiting for our flight, we noticed how close Mount Nyiragongo was to the city. Day and night the volcano menacingly belched out smoke. The locals told me that if it stopped smoking, everyone had better get ready for the next eruption. "Look, Dad, some of the UN planes are ready to take off," April pointed out. Bored by now, we had waited several hours for our late flight to arrive.

"I think they have to make room for the Hewa Bora plane to land. Maybe we'll see it soon," I answered. This was the first time I was flying with Hewa Bora Airlines. DRC had an unusual number of airline companies because much of the country is roadless. On other trips, I had flown with other airlines that offered cheaper fares. But now, Bravo Airline has gone bankrupt, and CAA had stopped flying due to mechanical problems with their airplane. I hoped the higher fare we paid for Hewa Bora meant that they are a safer airline. I didn't like flying in and out of Goma. Lava from the volcanic eruption in 2002 still covered more than a third of the runway. Now, as large planes landed, they had no margin for error. At the end of the runway ahead of them lay an unforgiving eight-foot-high wall of lava. Seven months earlier, a Russian-made cargo plane had failed to stop in time, and all eight crew members died in the crash.

After the fifth United Nations plane had taken off, we heard the roar of the DC-9 as our plane landed and taxied up to the terminal. People and luggage poured out of the plane that had left the capital city of Kinshasa early that morning and briefly stopped at Kisangani on its way to Goma.

"Let's go stand close to the door. Then we should be some of the first ones on the plane," I urged Marybeth and April.

Heavy rain clouds were coming our way, and it started to sprinkle as we walked across the tarmac. Marybeth tried to shield Andrew from the raindrops. We boarded the plane from the stairs at the tail section of the airplane. Being some of the first passengers, we had our choice of seats.

"Let's sit here next to the exit doors over the wings," I suggested. However, after we had stowed our heavy hand luggage and taken our seats, a frowning flight attendant stated, "Small children are not allowed to sit by the exit door."

"These seats are still available," observed Marybeth as we moved ahead two rows to the twelfth row. Sitting at the right window seat, April watched the rain come down in torrents. I sat directly on her left, watching the ground crew trying to cover the luggage that they had just unloaded from the plane.

Next to me sat an African businessman. Across the aisle sat Andrew at the window and Marybeth next to the aisle, that side of the plane having only two seats on each row. I took advantage of the rain delay to continue my memorization of the French days of the week. It had taken me eight years to learn Swahili, and I wondered if I could ever master another new language. I chatted briefly with the businessman.

"We're almost ready to take off. You must keep him in his seat belt," warned a flight attendant to Marybeth as she passed by. Andrew, excited, jumped around as we waited. Quickly, Marybeth fastened him in again for the third time.

Punching the numbers rapidly on my cell phone, I made a quick call to Keith. "Son, we are just taking off now. We'll see you in forty-five minutes."

"OK, Dad. I'll be there, and I can't wait to see you. I love you. Bye."

Slowly, the plane taxied into position with its back next to the wall of lava. The engines roared as the ancient DC-9 lumbered down the runway. The lava flow next to the runway became a blur as April and I stared out the window. The tired old plane shook as the speed increased. We anticipated being airborne any moment, but instead heard a loud *bang* from underneath the plane. We learned later that one of the two engines had failed. The pilot had only an instant to decide whether to continue to attempt takeoff or try to stop the plane. He later reported that the plane could have taken off, but probably would not have flown far. As he applied the brakes, the front tire blew out, creating a second *bang*. Could he stop this plane in time with so little remaining runway?

In the passenger section, we knew only that the pilot was trying to stop the plane. "Something's wrong," I said to April. My mind raced as I remembered that we took off over a lake. *How will we get out of here if we crash into the water?* I wondered to myself. Then, I remembered that Goma lay between us and the lake. *We will crash into the city,* I realized. Careening off the runway, the plane shook violently as we skidded across a vacant area covered with large boulders. The front wheel of the plane snapped off as we bumped over these huge rocks. Still traveling at a high speed, the plane now slid forward on its belly. Parts of the fuselage flew from the plane as it started to disintegrate. One woman's seat in the first-class section hooked on one of these boulders, and she died instantly when the momentum sucked her underneath the plane.

Next came a twenty-foot drop-off, below which were homes and an open-air market. The plane slowed as it smashed through the walls of these buildings.

Inside the plane, I knew we faced a violent crash. As I began to assume the brace position, the final impact came. All passengers jerked violently forward as the airplane finally came to a stop on top of the busy market. On impact, my glasses flew from my face, along with the cell phone from my shirt pocket. Immediately, I realized my glasses were missing and frantically started feeling the floor in front of me and under my seat to locate them.

"Dad, we've got to get out now!" April shouted as she unfastened her seat belt. Glancing up and across the aisle to where Marybeth and Andrew sat, I was horrified to see fire covering the wing. The fuel tanks on the wings had ruptured as the plane crashed through the buildings. Obviously, we faced a fiery death as the plane could explode at any second. As April reached the aisle, she joined the throng of people already clamoring toward the front of the plane. I instinctively started to follow her.

Trying to step into the aisle, I found my right foot trapped against the seat in front of me by the crush of passengers in the aisle. With a huge jerk, I wrenched my right foot loose, gashing my calf and leaving my right shoe behind. Looking across the aisle, I was shocked to see Marybeth still seated.

Dazed by a broken nose and without her glasses, she seemed to be living in a bad dream—a nightmare in slow motion. "Marybeth, give Andrew to me! We've got to get out of here!" I shouted back to her. Hearing Andrew's name alerted her, and she quickly handed him to me. Immediately, I again plunged into the avalanche of people pressing ahead.

A woman whose face was covered with blood grabbed me with both arms, screaming hysterically for help. Her face looked like a blur as smoke filled the cabin. I had plenty of my own problems as Andrew's dangling leg had become pinned between a broken seat and me by the shoving horde. Frantically, I tried twice to pull him out without hurting him, but couldn't seem to get any leverage. The thought *Run; get yourself out!* flashed through my mind. However, I never even considered this an option. Looking down at my adopted son, I knew that I could never leave him. If we were going to burn, we would burn together.

I looked up from Andrew's dilemma to see Marybeth in front of me. Somehow she had managed to crawl across the seatbacks to where I stood. As she saw the fire covering her side of the plane, she had prayed, *Lord, if it is my time to die, it's OK, but please make it quick!* Having worked as a nurse in burn units, she knew the torture of burns.

"Andrew's leg is stuck, and I can't get it out!" I shouted. Pulling from another angle, she mustered a mother's strength in a crisis. As she jerked him free, she snapped his femur bone in the process. As she pulled him free, I glanced down at my left hand and realized that I was still clutching the French notebook. In that split second, I realized that the notebook had made it harder for me to lift Andrew and could have cost both of us our lives. I flung it toward the front of the airplane in total disgust as I took Andrew back from Marybeth.

Almost immediately in front of us was a four-foot drop-off created when the plane broke up on impact. Now every breath became difficult as smoke poured into the plane. Outside, a wall of fire blazed on the left side of the plane. Without being able to see well, I feared to leap from the precipice to the broken floor below, so I leaned down and dropped Andrew onto an empty seat. He screamed when he landed as the pain from his broken leg stabbed through his body. Scrambling down to the lower section of seats, I had a vague recollection of seeing human arms and legs. Perhaps I saw people from the market who had been trapped under the plane, but I will never know for sure.

I continued stumbling through the wreckage, cradling Andrew in my arms. Time seemed to stand still as I fought my way through the smoke toward a large hole in the right side of the plane. As I reached the hole, a man stood outside with arms outstretched ready to take Andrew. After handing Andrew to him, I turned back to make sure Marybeth was coming. As she scrambled over the seats, she saw a man with his legs trapped under the broken seats. Fire had started to enter the cabin from under the plane. Filled with compassion, she strained several times to pull him free, but even a mother's strength could not win this battle.

As people pushed and shoved to try to get past her in the narrow aisle, she realized that her efforts might be preventing other people from getting to safety. So, with an aching heart, she left him to flee toward the gaping hole in the side of the plane. We met as I struggled back against the crowd to make sure she was coming.

Quickly, we jumped the short distance to the ground and fled across the street. We needed to put some distance between us and the airplane, which could explode any time. Surely, the Lord had intervened to keep it from exploding. Even as we glanced back, three massive explosions occurred over the midsection of the plane. We doubted that anyone got out after that.

We were alive, but where were April and Andrew? Had April gotten out alive?

Chapter 2
FIRST TASTE OF AFRICA

As a boy, my early interest in Africa centered more on elephants, lions, giraffes, and other wild animals than in telling others about Jesus. Nonetheless, the fascination remained. Seeing photos of ebony warriors in plumed headgear dancing round a fire and waving spears captured my imagination. I dreamed of going to Africa to see these wonders.

However, growing up with three sisters and a brother in the rural Minnesota town of Redwood Falls, I found that my world was pretty small. My father, Harold, a carpenter and an avid outdoorsman, expressed little interest in religion until his later years. He often took me hunting and fishing and gave me an enduring love for the outdoors. Each Sabbath while he went hunting or fishing, my mother, Viola, packed us all into the car and drove us to church in a nearby town.

I still remember at age eight traveling the unbelievable distance of sixty miles to attend my first camp meeting at Hutchinson, Minnesota. There I saw my first African American family. I stared at their black skin and curly hair in wonder. I had never before seen anybody who looked like them. I watched their every move. Looking back now after spending eight years in Africa, I have been well repaid for my discourteous youthful staring. People in remote villages have stared holes through me more times than I can count, but I understand. They have never before seen anybody with white skin and straight hair like mine. They watch my every move.

Anyway, the mission stories told over the years in Sabbath School had their effect. By the time I attended Union College in my junior year, I longed to volunteer as a student missionary in order to serve

Jesus in some faraway place. However, the cost was far beyond my budget.

Also, I didn't want to be away from Marybeth for an entire year. I had known her since Cradle Roll class in Sabbath School. In those days, she irritated me because she could easily outrun me. Time changes things, and by the time I reached Union College, she had become the girl of my dreams.

When I asked her to marry me, I made a fundamental error. Somehow, an *if* slipped into the proposal. Maybe I tried to soften the blow in case she said No. "If I asked you to marry me, would you say Yes?" I stammered.

"Well, are you asking or aren't you?" she demanded, wanting a clear commitment on my part.

"Yes, I'm asking," I weakly replied as I kicked myself for not being braver.

"OK, then my answer is Yes," she clearly responded.

Halleluiah! Poor start, great response! Thrilled, I felt like the luckiest guy in the world. So we started married life hoping to use our professions to win people to God, Marybeth as a registered nurse and me as a certified public accountant. Although I had applied for work in a number of places before Marybeth's graduation, we waited for God's directions. One day after praying earnestly about where we should go, I felt impressed to call Myrna Bowie, the Adventist CPA in Dodge Center, Minnesota. When I interviewed with her earlier, she had no openings.

"Hello, Mrs. Bowie. This is Barry Mosier. I know that you didn't have any openings for employment, but I'm just checking to see if there have been any changes."

"It's amazing that you should call," she responded. "Just today one of my accountants had to quit for reasons beyond her control. Yes. I have an opening today."

Taking this as God's providence, we readily accepted the position. Myrna, an outstanding accountant, patiently taught me the public accounting profession, and in 1980, we formed a partnership called Bowie & Mosier, Certified Public Accountants.

Marybeth and I soon had three children to rear on our fifty-acre farm near Dodge Center. Our daughter, Laura, helped in managing her two younger brothers, Keith and Jared. And Marybeth became a homeschooling mother.

The children loved to "surprise" me on my way home from work. With great anticipation, they would walk down the quiet gravel road that passed by our home and hide in the tall grass in the ditch. Then, as my car approached, they would jump up and wave their arms and shout, "Daddy, Daddy!" Of course, they climbed into the car and rode the rest of the way home with me, telling me all the adventures of the day.

We enjoyed living in the country with our big garden and walks through the woods. Jared loved to tell me the location of every new bird nest that he found. The books *The Adventist Home* and *Child Guidance* became invaluable guides to us as we sought to rear our children to honor God.

The Dodge Center church inspired us. The McNeilus family, involved with both church-sponsored and self-supporting ministries from around the world, brought a steady stream of missionaries to share their testimonies about God's work. Stories from Japan, Cambodia, Russia, and Brazil thrilled our souls. I felt deeply grateful to Pat McNeilus, who invited me to accompany him in attending the annual Adventist Laymen's Services and Industries (ASI) meeting in Big Sky, Montana, in 1984. This unveiled to me another world of the many supporting ministries connected to the Adventist Church. Our family began the practice of reading mission story books in the evenings at home.

On a hot August Sabbath in 1992, we met Kim and Joyce Busl and their two boys from Riverside Farm Institute in Zambia, Africa. Their stories and slides that morning fanned some old embers in my heart for Africa. We invited them for an afternoon visit to our home. As Kim surveyed our simple home and large garden, he said, "I think you are the kind of people who would do well in Africa. We have several small mission outposts where we need someone to train them to do accounting. Do you think you and your family could come and help us for a few months sometime?"

"Maybe," I replied as I tried to contain my excitement. After more discussions, we decided to go the following summer. We wanted more than just a two week "honeymoon" mission experience. We wanted to know what it was really like to live in another country, so we planned a three-month trip beginning July 1993.

We landed in Lusaka, Zambia, eager to experience Africa. As we passed into the baggage-claim area of the airport, a tall, sandy-haired man greeted us.

"You must be the Mosiers. I'm Alan Knowles from Riverside. The vehicle broke down on its way to collect you. Don't worry. Another one will soon come."

We soon loaded all of our things onto two carts. Laura and Keith each leaped at the chance to push one of the carts and promptly got stuck in the door as both tried to pass through it at the same time. Two men moved swiftly to "help" us free the carts. In the confusion, I saw Alan snatch his satchel from the hand of one of the men.

In the parking lot I asked, "What happened? Why did you grab your satchel away from those men? Weren't they just trying to help us?"

"No," he laughed. "They are thieves. They had taken my satchel from the top of your bags and were making their getaway. This is your first lesson here. Some people who look like they are trying to help you are really helping themselves."

On the way to Riverside Farm, we tried to soak everything in as we gazed out the windows. Third-world conditions amazed us on our first trip outside the United States. One sight made an indelible impression on me. I saw a man sitting in the hot sun with a hammer, breaking large rocks into piles of crushed rock to sell. All day. Every day. Almost like stories about prisoners getting a sentence of twenty years of hard labor on the rock pile. But this man hadn't done anything wrong! I tried to imagine being the son of this man on the day when he would say, "Son, someday all this will be yours!" I had never before seen poverty and need like this.

We soon learned to fit into the daily mission activities. What friendly people! I taught bookkeeping classes to the African leaders. My mother, Viola, accompanied us on our trip to Africa, and soon she and Marybeth planted a garden. On the ninth day of our stay, we stood on the high escarpment overlooking the campus. We exclaimed at the breathtaking view of the crops below us and the curve of the Kafue River, which provided irrigation for the project. As we descended the escarpment, Laura complained about feeling sick to her stomach and having a mild headache. "Sounds like malaria symptoms," stated Pauline Knowles. "We'll test your blood right away."

When the test confirmed malaria, Marybeth and I glanced at each other nervously. After only nine days, our thirteen-year-old daughter had a killer disease. For the next three days, she took the course of Chloriquine medicine. During that time, the poison killed the parasites in her bloodstream. Not until three more days did she regain her strength. Before the end of our time in Zambia, most of us experienced malaria firsthand.

Time flew by as we helped with bush clinics, traveled to remote projects, and attended branch Sabbath Schools. Alan and Pauline Knowles involved us in many aspects of mission life. At the bush clinic in Luyando, I helped weigh babies while Marybeth and Laura administered immunizations. My mother recorded the babies' weights while Keith and Jared weighed out the food for underweight babies. At the camp meeting, we saw people giving their lives to Jesus and requesting baptism. At the prison, we gave out tracts and prayed with people who lived in the most pitiful conditions.

Frankly, I never had had so much fun in my life. The African people got into my heart in a way that I cannot describe. Sylvester and Unity Temboh typified the Zambian workers. Their big smiles and friendliness proved genuine, as they happily served Jesus. I little dreamed that Sylvester and I would work together ten years later at Kibidula Farm.

During the last three weeks of our stay, we planned to travel to Kibidula Farm Institute in Tanzania with Kim Busl and his family. Traveling through Malawi, we made the entire trip in three days. As we crossed the Malawi border into Tanzania, we raced the clock to reach Kibidula before nightfall. Border agents can easily detain travelers, and we held our breath as they inspected the luggage. Keith picked that very moment to play a joke. Pointing to one of our long army surplus packs, he said to the customs officer, "That pack is where we hid all the guns."

Of course, we did not have a single gun with us, and why he chose to say such a thing, I will never know. We looked at the officer, wondering how many hours it would take to sort this out.

The officer narrowed his eyes a bit and looked directly at Keith. "You are a very naughty boy," he said as he waved us through. We let out a sigh of relief as we crossed the border and gave Keith a little instruction about what *not* to say the next time.

Kim talked to us as he drove. "The African people really like you and your family. We want to give you a call to come and work here." Marybeth and I agreed to pray about it and see how the Lord led.

At Kibidula, they neared the end of a six-month dry season by mid-September. We were not prepared for the cool fifty-degree nights and windy, dusty days. Still recovering from my latest bout of malaria, I got food poisoning in a Malawi restaurant on the way. Both Keith and Laura came down with malaria shortly after we arrived. However, during our stay, we had the privilege of seeing 140 people baptized during the Kibidula church camp meeting.

We prayed earnestly about the invitation to work in Africa. It would be a big step for us to pack up our family and move to Africa. Although we knew that God would make it clear to us, the answer that came surprised us.

Chapter 3
PLANS DELAYED

Back in Minnesota, Marybeth's father, Bud Burghart, suffered a stroke in early November after being diagnosed with Alzheimer's disease in October. "Marybeth, I cannot handle your father anymore." Marybeth's mother sounded desperate on the phone. "Could you come and help me and maybe take Bud to your house for a while?"

"Sure, Mom, I'll be there in a few hours," replied Marybeth. The next day, Marybeth brought Grandpa home to live with us. However, he no longer seemed to be the same Grandpa Burghart we knew. On the second day, I got a desperate phone call from Marybeth. "Can you come home and help me get Dad into the car so I can take him to the hospital? He just tore one of the phones off the wall, because he suspected me of talking about him on the telephone. He's so confused."

On the way home, I realized that Marybeth's father must be our first consideration. Apparently, God's answer to our prayers about moving to Africa was either, "No, or Not now."

Grandpa's condition steadily deteriorated. Finally, with great sadness, we were forced to put him into the Dodge Center Nursing Home, where we continued to watch over him.

As business continued to increase and homeschool consumed much of Marybeth's time, Africa faded from our minds again. During this time, a little newborn named April Rose arrived in our home. Marybeth was thrilled to have a baby in our home again.

In the late 1990s, another missionary from Kibidula started to make an annual visit to Dodge Center. As he shared his stories of bush evangelism and the publishing work, God stirred my heart again.

In the Dodge Center area, we shared our faith with neighbors and clients. We felt gratified as the Lord blessed our efforts, and we saw a number of people choose to be baptized. Laura took some classes at the local community college before attending Union College, and over time her adventures with her community-college classmates brought four of them to our home for Friday-evening Bible studies. When we finally took Laura to Union College in Nebraska, one of those friends, Gretchen, went with us to see the college. She was so impressed that she decided to enroll also! The Holy Spirit worked uniquely in each of their lives, and eventually all four were baptized. Seeing people choose to join the Adventist Church and come to know Jesus more fully thrilled our souls with satisfaction and joy.

A verse in Isaiah kept tugging at my mind day after day. Isaiah 55:2 says, "Wherefore do ye spend money for that which is not bread? and your labour for that which satisfieth not?" Although I enjoyed my accounting work and my clients, I felt a desire to work more directly for God full time. I believed He could bless my labor with satisfying results that would endure for eternity.

In the fall of 1998, I attended a three-week evangelism training course at Mission College of Evangelism. After returning to Minnesota, Marybeth and I were taking a walk through the woods near our home one evening just after dark. A thin crescent of a moon was just rising, and the stars twinkled overhead. We talked about God's will for us and whether He might be calling us to do something different. "Marybeth, I wonder whether we did the right thing when we turned down Kim's call to Africa," I pondered. The word *Africa* had no sooner passed my lips than a flash appeared on the left horizon and flashed all across the sky to the right horizon. I saw the most brilliant shooting star that I had ever seen.

"Wow, I wonder what that was supposed to mean?" I said.

"I don't know, but for sure God was trying to tell us something important," Marybeth responded in awe.

At the end of a particularly busy week that tax season, a letter came from Rudy Harnisch. At the end of the letter, he wrote, "We desperately need help here at Kibidula, and every time we pray, your name comes up." Although that Friday evening was very cold, I hardly noticed as I walked through the snow, praying for direction. That night we decided to step out in faith and join the work at Kibidula as volunteers.

We faced a major test to our faith. Was God preparing us for the last days? I am not a giant of faith, but God gives me strength when I am weak. As we followed God's calling, we sometimes saw only darkness ahead with no path for our feet. However, as we moved forward in faith, God amazed us when we looked back to see where He directed us. We seemed to see a four-lane highway where the Lord led the way. As we faced trials or felt confused, we learned to trust completely in God. Going as volunteers, we could not expect any salary. We decided to rent out our house to cover our living costs in Africa.

Marybeth found security in our peaceful home and fifty-acre farm in the country. For fifteen years she raised her family in the comforts of this home. Each tree and flower became her precious friend. Special memories called to her from every birdhouse and fence post. Selling the pet horses and dogs was painful, but God gave her inner strength to move forward in faith.

As my old pickup chugged out of the driveway with a new owner behind the wheel, I turned to Marybeth and said, "Well, that's about the last thing to go. Honey, I stopped at the mall yesterday. Wow, I won't miss this media blitz that hammers people every day here in America. People are becoming so numb to the influence of sin."

"Yes, it's easy to say Goodbye to some things," Marybeth sighed. "But not to Laura. She's only twenty now and still has two years to finish in her nursing degree at Union College. At least she can visit Grandma or my brother, Mark, during school breaks. I'm going to miss her so much and will pray for her a lot."

Two days later, on May 5, 2000, when we landed in Dar es Salaam (Dar) in Tanzania, we were met by a familiar face. "It's sure good to see you folks," chuckled Rudy Harnisch with his contagious laugh. After a nine-hour drive, the towering eucalyptus trees and scenic views of Kibidula Mission greeted us. We worked quickly to settle in before nightfall. The blankets felt good as we snuggled into our beds that night. May was the beginning of the cold, dry season, where the six-thousand-foot elevation provided very cool nights.

We had a lot to learn in those early days before our container arrived. Cooking meals and heating bath water on a charcoal burner were new experiences for Marybeth. Oh, how she missed the cooking pots and supplies that would come on the container, but she maintained her missionary spirit. The little stream about thirty feet from our door provided our wash water.

Jared, deeply disappointed to leave friends and home behind, adapted to the environment and people the fastest. While the rest of us struggled to master a few words in Swahili, he seemed to absorb the language. Colporteurs walked the eight miles from the main road to Rudy's home almost every day to purchase books. Keith and Jared helped sell books and gave the colporteurs rides back to the main road on a four-wheeler.

Within a few days, Jason Harral and his friend Josh Marcoe returned to Kibidula from their church-measuring trip. They had traveled extensively, helping Rudy with the Roofs Over Africa program and also the distribution of bicycles to gospel workers. Josh's ingenuity helped him navigate his way around Tanzania with a limited

The Mosier family after their arrival in Africa in September 2000.

Swahili vocabulary. We had known Jason as a Bible worker in the Dodge Center area, where we had shared many great times together. He preceded us by three months in coming to Kibidula. Both of these young men were integral parts of our gospel team. When Keith played guitar for our evening praise sessions, we felt that heaven was very near.

Littered with termite mounds, the grasslands of Kibidula were turning brown and resembled fields of wheat in the wind. The straw flowers had bloomed and now dried in the warm, sunny days of May. The freshwater springs of our upper campus joined together to form streams that carved out the beautiful valleys of Kibidula. These streams fed the huge marsh that looks like a huge grassy meadow. Dignified herons dotted the marsh as they fished in their white wedding clothes. As we stood overlooking the lovely marsh meadow below us, we knew God had placed us where He wanted us to serve Him.

However, we soon found out that the work would not always be easy.

Chapter 4
INITIATION

One day in the mid-1990s, Rudy noticed some dusty boxes of books in a back room at Kibidula. Opening them, he found they contained copies of *The Great Controversy*. Placing them on a sale rack at the Kibidula lumberyard in Mafinga, he noticed how quickly they sold. Knowing of the acute book shortage for literature evangelists in Tanzania, Rudy made up his mind to try to assist the publishing work. Rudy longed to get Swahili books into the hands of the ordinary people.

Hiring a translator, Rudy had many key articles by Ellen G. White translated into Swahili. Light Bearers Ministry in the United States of America printed and shipped containers of Swahili tracts and booklets. Rudy also purchased Swahili books from the Adventist Press in Kenya. Soon literature evangelists streamed to Kibidula to purchase books to sell. Then, conflicts developed over prices and territory. Soon the conflict grew into a major issue between Kibidula and publishing leaders.

We prayed earnestly before meeting with church leaders in Morogoro. Although some leaders expressed strong negative feelings in the meetings, others seemed willing to compromise and cooperate. With this encouraging start, we felt confident that God would help us solve the conflict.

Late in May, Rudy, Jared, and I left in the Unimog truck for Nairobi to collect books that had been printed at the Africa Herald Press in Kendu Bay, northern Kenya. On the way we stopped in Same to deliver religious tracts and bicycles for workers in the North-East Tanzania Conference. The bicycles would benefit pastors and colporteurs in their evangelistic work. The church leaders greeted us with great enthusiasm.

"What do you want to be when you grow up?" asked Pastor Mambwe of Jared as we sat eating our lunch together.

"I want to be a bush pilot," Jared replied honestly.

"A what?" responded the pastor.

"A pilot that flies people into the bush," Jared answered again.

This answer seemed to tickle that group of pastors, and they have never forgotten it. Even after eight years, if they want to inquire about Jared, they still ask me how my bush pilot is doing.

The next day we headed toward Nairobi, Kenya. Passing through the grazing lands of the Maasai people, we were shocked by the results of the severe drought in that area. The sky darkened as huge wind-swept clouds of dust enveloped our truck. In the distance, we faintly distinguished the ghostlike figures of herdsmen driving large herds of starving cattle in a vain attempt to find food for them. We couldn't see a blade of grass.

"Why don't they sell the cattle and salvage what they can?" I asked Rudy.

"You don't understand. Cattle are the Maasai's bank accounts. Selling them all is unthinkable. They will watch most of them die as they hope against hope for rain," Rudy replied. The starving animals were a pitiful sight.

Incredibly, after only three weeks in the country, Jared could already help us with some translation. We managed to cross the border just before dark, but still had far to go to reach Nairobi. We continued to travel along at forty-two miles per hour, the cruising speed of the Unimog truck. "Watch out!" shouted Jared as his keen eyes detected a movement in front us. Rudy hit the brakes just as a large kudu buck leaped across the road in front of us. "Whew, that was close. Proves the angels travel with us," commented Rudy as we continued on into the night.

The next day in Nairobi, we loaded the truck with ten thousand Swahili books. That day, Reuben arrived by bus to join us before Sabbath. As Rudy's right-hand man, he would help us to clear the books at the border customs office on our return trip. Saturday night the leaders of the press at Kendu Bay phoned and pleaded with Rudy to return the next day by a shuttle airplane for a very important meeting. They assured us that we would be able to get back the same day by plane, so I agreed to accompany him, leaving Jared in Nairobi with Reuben.

The meeting about their need to increase prices significantly, followed by lengthy discussions, finally ended with an agreement. After purchasing more books from them, we waited for the pickup to take us back to the airport in Kisumu. We waited and waited. I became very anxious since I had left Jared in Nairobi, known as a very dangerous city.

When we arrived at the airport, we were informed that the plane was full. "But you guaranteed us a return flight today!" I complained to no avail.

"Sorry," answered the ticket agent. Quickly we hurried to the bus stand and managed to get tickets on an overnight bus to Nairobi. Although the bus appeared to be in poor condition, we decided we had no other choice. We prayed that the Lord would protect us on the way. The bad condition of Kenya's roads kept us awake all night as we bounced along toward Nairobi.

I praised the Lord as we pulled into the downtown Nairobi bus stand at 3:00 A.M. "Rudy, why is no one getting off the bus?" I asked when not a single passenger moved.

"Not even the Africans will get off in this dangerous section of town at night. However, let's try and get a taxi to take us to our hotel. What do you say?"

"Let's pray, Rudy. I believe the Lord has cared for us up to now."

Exiting the bus, we walked a couple of blocks before waking up a taxi driver. Finally back at the hotel, I was overjoyed to see that Jared was safe. I vowed to myself that I would never leave a thirteen-year-old child without his parents so far from home again.

We reached the dirty border town of Namanga that afternoon. Reuben had remained behind in Nairobi to start the clearing process for our books. Crossing borders is always a challenge, especially with cargo. After clearing the books in only a few hours, I praised God as we drove past the line of trucks that had been stuck there at the border for many days. In Arusha late that night, we met up with Josh Marcoe, who was measuring churches for roofs in that area.

The next day, Rudy teamed up with Josh, while Jared and I caught a bus to Dar. Thieves infest the Arusha bus station, so we watched our bags alertly as we waited for Josh to return with the tickets. Six men began to approach us noisily, pointing at us and our bags. "Dad, I don't like the actions of these guys. Maybe they plan to rob us," Jared confided quietly.

"Let's pray, Jared," I said as we bowed our heads in prayer for God's protection.

Just as we raised our heads, Josh Marcoe appeared around the corner, and the men stared in his direction chattering loudly and rapidly among themselves. We will never know if they saw a troop of guards with Josh, but they left quickly. Soon, a tall policeman came and stood near us until we boarded the bus. Our angels stayed close to us.

The next day in Dar, we worked on clearing our container from America through customs. Another forty-footer also had arrived, filled with books and supplies for Kibidula. No single thing in Africa causes more headaches than clearing containers through customs. The corrupt process filled with unreasonable demands and extra costs is most frustrating.

When Rudy arrived late the following day, we decided our trip had been long enough. In spite of the late hour, we started for Kibidula. We arrived home at 5:00 A.M. the next morning, exhausted. I had completed my first long trip in Africa. God had cared for us all along the way.

Another trip to Morogoro the next week brought more breakthroughs, more goodwill, and a voted agreement between publishing leaders and Kibidula. We realized that only with a spirit of cooperation between us could we satisfy the great need for books in Tanzania. Getting the truths out through our publications was more important than focusing on petty issues. Working cooperatively was the only solution.

Anxious to head home after these meetings, I waited in vain for an empty seat on one of the passing buses. Finally, I chose to take a spot on the floor rather than wait another day. I bought a bag of pineapples from the vendors as a treat for my family. The driver drove much too fast, speeding around the corners on our way through the mountains. The trees outside the windows became a green blur as the bus swayed from side to side. I clung to the seats on either side of me from my spot on the floor. Eventually my stomach rebelled, and my breakfast came back up. I continued to retch into the bag of pineapples as my fellow passengers watched with interest the poor sick *mzungu* (white person) on the floor. I hoped that one of them would take pity on me and offer to share a part of his seat, but not until late in the trip did a seat became available. Was this God's way to teach me patience?

I arrived in time to see Keith, Josh, Jason, and Reuben busy packing. They left the following Sunday for a big evangelistic series in Shinyanga, three days' travel in the Unimog. Keith, only seventeen, seemed thrilled to be part of the team. Four and a half weeks would transpire before we would see him again.

Marybeth was glad to have me home for three weeks. She explained, "Barry, I'm not accustomed to your doing all this travel. I feel quite trapped when I'm alone without you." In a new country with limited language skills—and no phone, car, electricity, or husband at home—the days had been pretty long.

"Honey, I'm glad I can take a break from travel for a while now," I replied.

Three weeks later, a major series of evangelistic meetings began in Dar. Church publishing leaders asked us to sell books there, an opportunity to sell books under the new agreement. We had recently decided to sell the old Kenworth truck also. We decided to combine the two trips. Jason Fournier, our lumberyard manager, loaded the Kenworth and all the books onto the International truck. Then, together with Jared and me, began the all-night drive to Dar.

Trying to make our roof-sheet program more efficient, we set up a new plan to purchase sheets in large quantities in Dar and ship them to regional locations. This would allow us to do major amounts of church roofing in a short time for the Roofs Over Africa program. When I returned to Kibidula, Keith had arrived too. He told many stories of their adventures and the people who had been won to Christ in Shinyanga.

At the end of July, our container arrived at Kibidula. Hurray! After unloading it, we turned it into a shop and storage facility next to our house. We celebrated as if it were Christmas as the things we had carefully packed came into view again! The top priorities in unpacking were the wood-burning cookstove for our kitchen and the solar power unit. How we rejoiced as we looked forward to the conveniences those items would supply.

Chapter 5

OUR PERSONAL MIRACLE

Although from the beginning we expected Satan to try to discourage us, the blow took us by surprise when it hit. Building a gate to our courtyard to accommodate the vehicle that was soon to come, we needed a load of sand for the cement. Since a villager also needed two loads, Yesse, our Kibidula tractor driver, decided to attempt all three loads in one day from the village of Kisada, about eight miles away. For something interesting to do, Jared opted to ride along with the tractor and trailer. The first two loads went well, but after the second load, they relaxed with a soda and some *mandazi* (cakes). By the time they started out for the third load, they were running late.

Jared sat in a safe half seat next to the wheel well. The days began to warm up as spring approached on that second day of August. However, the breeze felt cool as Yesse tried to make up for lost time with high speed. Jared held on tightly as the tractor bounced over the bumpy roads. The two-wheel trailer made of solid steel, extremely big and heavy, rumbled along behind them. Its weight helped push them down the bumpy hill as they approached the village of Bumalainga. A stream trickled by on the left and a cornfield lay to the right. Just before the road started climbing again into the village, they hit a big bump. As Yesse landed back on his seat, he turned the steering wheel to the left to keep control of the tractor. As he did so, the steering wheel came off the shaft. Frantically, he tried to jam the wheel back onto the shaft, but regaining control of the tractor was impossible.

Another rut in the road jerked the front wheels to the right, and the tractor left the road and headed for the ditch beside the road. The heavy trailer followed behind them. Crossing the ditch, the tractor bounced mightily, like a bucking bronco trying to shake off its riders. Jared hung on for life as the tractor barreled into the cornfield.

Directly in front of them, a heavy tree branch hung menacingly. Striking Jared in the chest, it knocked him violently off the tractor, flipping him midair. The right side of his head landed heavily on the hard ground, and a cornstalk jammed into his nostril on the impact. His head lay directly in the path of the huge trailer wheel.

Then, at that crucial moment, Jared's guardian angel stopped the tractor. Yesse saw Jared fall in front of the trailer wheel. He claimed that he stopped the tractor with the brakes. We know that was impossible. Only a guardian angel could have stopped the tractor, still traveling rapidly and pulling the heavy trailer, before it hit Jared. Yesse himself was slammed against the steering wheel with such force that his ribs hurt for three weeks afterward. Only a miracle from God saved our son's life.

Immediately, Yesse leaped from the tractor to help Jared. Blood poured out his nose and onto his face, and the side of his head started to swell rapidly. Jared started to revive as a kind old woman helped Yesse wash the blood from his face. His first recollections were of a woman's callused, dirt-covered hands pouring cool water over his head from an old cracked plastic jug. The numbness turned to pain as Jared started to realize his serious injuries. Terrified and confused, he leaped to his feet and started to run across the field.

Yesse quickly caught him and grabbed him. "Jared!" he shouted.

"Are you Yesse?" Jared asked in confusion.

"Yes. I am Yesse. You'll be OK."

"Yesse, my head is broken! My head is broken!" screamed Jared in panic as he collapsed into Yesse's arms weeping uncontrollably.

"No, Jared. Your head is not broken. You will be OK. Just rest a bit, and we will get you home."

Just at that time, Valentino, our Kibidula night watchman, passed by. "Let me use your bicycle to take Jared home to his father. He's hurt and needs help," asked Yesse.

Taking Yesse aside, Valentino replied, "No. His father will kill you when he sees the boy's condition. Let me take him home."

"Yes, you're right," agreed Yesse as he helped place Jared onto the bicycle and watched Valentino pedal rapidly away. Jared felt himself passing out several times over the next five miles toward home. He wondered if he would ever be the same again and also about the extent of his injuries.

About 3:00 P.M., our house worker Salome ran from the house screaming, "Jared *anakufa*! Jared *anakufa*! [Jared is dying!]" As we ran to the door, Jared stumbled in saying, "Mom and Dad, I'm OK, but I think my jaw is broken in two places."

"Jared, what happened?" exclaimed Marybeth as she gazed at his disfigured face, hardly recognizable from the injured side. Quickly we seated him on the sofa.

"The tractor crashed, and now my mouth doesn't work right anymore." We could see that his jaw hung at an odd angle on his face.

"Let's take him up to Dr. Sparks's house to see what he thinks we should do," I said as we headed for the four-wheeler. Both Steven Sparks and his wife, Kathleen, were physicians. Steven was gone, but Kathleen gave Jared a quick examination at her door, and said, "You need to take him to a hospital. You might go to a good one near Songea, but Dar would be better, in case you have to go to Nairobi for reconstructive surgery on his jaw," she explained sympathetically.

We raced back home to throw some things together for the trip, leaving Keith in charge of April. As we prepared to leave, Jason Fournier came up to the old Mazda pickup, "Can I drive you to Dar?" he asked.

"That would be such a blessing. We don't know where to go after we get there," I replied with a sense of relief. After a prayer, we started the journey.

As we drove through the night, the vehicle started to cough and sputter. "What's wrong?" I asked Jason as we pulled off the road. "I don't know. The motor acts like it's starving for fuel," replied Jason as he analyzed the situation.

"I'm sure glad you're along," I said considering my own lack of mechanical ability. "Let's pray again." We bowed our heads as we called helplessly on our heavenly Father.

Jason shut off the ignition, and when he started it again, the engine purred like a kitten. Our journey continued. Several times we had to stop for Jared to throw up the blood that had drained into his stomach. Several times more the little truck sputtered and stalled. Each time Jason turned off the ignition. Then, when he started it again, the engine purred. We prayed along the way and praised God for His care for us. After only eight and a half hours, we pulled into Aga Khan Hospital just after midnight.

Nurses put Jared in a wheelchair and took him into the emergency room. Through the darkened halls they wheeled him to the X-ray department to take X-rays of his head. "Father, we trust in You," we prayed while we waited for the X-ray results. "You are the Divine Physician. Please heal our son. Amen."

As the doctor returned, he smiled and said, "I have good news for you. I found no broken bones. However, with a head injury like this, he must stay in the hospital for observation for a few days."

Our mouths must have dropped open as Marybeth and I looked first at each other and then at Jared. "It's not possible," Marybeth exclaimed in disbelief as she looked closely at Jared's face. "Look! Look!" She cried incredulously, "His jaw is straight."

As Jared worked his jaw in a chewing motion, Marybeth said reverently, "Jared, God answered our prayers and healed your jaw. Praise His name!"

That night as we looked out the hospital window at the stars in the sky, we poured out our hearts in grateful thanks to God. The swelling in Jared's head diminished steadily, and after four days, he was discharged from the hospital. A CT scan taken some months later revealed that a small bone below his eye had been broken, but had since healed itself. God had taken certain disaster and turned it to good.

God wanted to save another Son many years ago. Although it wounded His Father-heart terribly to watch His Son die a painful death, He couldn't save both Him and you and me. Out of God's love for you and me, He let His own Son die to save us. I'm so grateful for that kind of love. Nevertheless, my heart overflows with thankfulness and praise that He chose to intervene and save our son's life. "He shall give his angels charge over thee, to keep thee in all thy ways" (Psalm 91:11).

Chapter 6
REMEMBER TO PRAY

Godfrey Sanga, the patriarch of Kibidula, now seventy years old, had served as house boy for the original owner of the property before they donated it to the Seventh-day Adventist Church. He still retained his youthful enthusiasm and love of the gospel, a huge help to Kibidula. He and Jason had just finished an evangelistic meeting in a small town and had built a church in the mountains of Makete, Godfrey's home area. Now, Keith and Jason prepared to leave and construct the second church. Jason had become a positive influence on Keith. They both loved winning souls and formed an excellent team.

Although we had arrived at 1:30 A.M. the night before from our ambulance trip to Dar, Marybeth and I went to Mafinga to make some phone calls and buy needed groceries. In one of the calls, Rudy Harnisch gave us good news from America. Generous people had donated fifteen thousand dollars for a publishing vehicle and also nine thousand dollars for evangelism. We praised God for this providence!

But Rudy had more news. "People you know have donated money for a new staff house at Kibidula. They want you to build it and live in it," Rudy explained. Marybeth and I were shocked. Tired from the trip to Dar after Jared's accident, I whispered in an aside to Marybeth, "Building a house will only slow down God's work. Besides that, I don't know how to build in Africa."

Marybeth suggested, "Since our container came, we're quite comfortable in the old Busl house. I hate to say No to a gift, because I know they have our best interests at heart, but let's just call one of them now and tell them that we don't need the house."

As we tried to explain the reasons to one of the donors, the answer came back, "Oh yes, you do need a new house, and so does Kibidula. The institution is growing, and another staff house will be very helpful in the future. You are going to build that house, and you are going to live in it!" After a long uncomfortable pause on the phone, I replied, "Thank you. We will build the house," I saw no other option.

Since that day, we have praised the Lord many times for the wisdom of our friends. As they read our e-mails, they could see that without a comfortable home in which to rest from our work and travel, we would quickly burn out. The new house became an oasis many times over the years. Truly, that home became a blessing to Kibidula as well. "Where no counsel is, the people fall: but in the multitude of counsellors there is safety" (Proverbs 11:14).

Another blessing followed quickly. A few days after the news of the new house, Josh drove in with the used van we had ordered from Japan. In America, we were used to having access to a vehicle at any time. Now we had a vehicle again! Marybeth felt like a woman set free!

The following week, our family left for a short vacation. We needed a break and planned to take a visit to Zanzibar. Jason Harral and Josh Marcoe accompanied us. We enjoyed a great time. Fantastic snorkeling and three relaxing days at the beach gave us a refreshing break from work. One day, the boys rented three motorcycles and circled the island.

We had come prepared to hand out literature, in spite of the fact that Zanzibar is almost exclusively Muslim and very conservative. As we headed into the town after a season of prayer, people readily accepted the literature. However, by the time we retraced our steps about half an hour later, several women fled from us in fear. Someone had turned us in. We immediately returned to our hotel. Naively, I thought no one would be upset by a family of tourists discreetly handing out literature for so short a time. However, I did know that Christian men had been severely beaten or killed in the past for doing evangelism on Zanzibar.

Jason and Jared were delayed in their return, and we prayed for their safety. Finally, they returned to the hotel, eager to tell about their experience. "Most of the people in the mosque accepted our literature," Jared said innocently. My eyes widened in amazement, "What? You mean to say you gave tracts out in the mosque? That's a very risky thing to do."

"They didn't give us any trouble, and who knows what these seeds of truth may accomplish," replied Jason with a smile.

When Rudy and I had earlier visited the Africa Herald Publishing House in Kenya, the manager sadly showed us their broken generator that provided the power to run their printing presses. "We fear we might have to close down unless something happens soon."

"How can we lose another lighthouse in Africa?" I had answered. "Unthinkable. Another light cannot go out!"

With money Rudy raised in America, we purchased a high-quality used generator in Dar from a church member. We began preparations to deliver the generator to Kenya with our big truck.

That Monday morning we met for breakfast in our room to divide up the duties for the day. We shared our long list of duties between three teams. This day seemed most important. Right after breakfast we quickly left, with each team gathering their things for the day. Soon everyone had left. My team, last to leave, rushed all the more. Not once did it occur to me that we had not taken time to lay all our plans before the throne of God.

"Hey, isn't that where our van was parked?" I gasped as I saw the heavy black trail of oil leading out the gate onto the street. "Josh must have left just a few minutes ago. Maybe we can still catch him before they run out of oil!" I shouted as I raced to find a taxi.

"Follow that stream of oil," I ordered the taxi driver in the best Swahili I could muster. We followed the thick oil trail easily for the first two blocks. At the first major intersection, the driver looked at me as if to say, "Where do we go now?" Our van must not have been the only vehicle in town that leaked oil. We saw a neat trail of oil going to the left and another neat trail going to the right. Since Josh had duties in both directions, I had no idea which duties he intended to do first. "*Kata kushoto* [Turn left]," I said with a sickening feeling in the pit of my stomach as I tried to guess which way he turned.

By the time we reached the destination to the left, I realized we followed the wrong trail. Having wasted twenty minutes, all I could think was *Have we destroyed the engine of the van after owning it for only two weeks?* I had paid eight thousand dollars of my own money for it and could hardly bear to think of such a loss. As we slowly returned to the intersection through the heavy traffic, my hopes languished. By now Josh could have driven far away, but what could I do but try to find him? In those days, we had no cell phones like Africa enjoys today to make communication simple.

Finally, in my extremity, I called on my heavenly Father to help me.

Not until late morning did we finally catch up with Josh. The trail of oil had long since vanished. I wondered how much oil would be left. "You have an oil leak in the van," I announced as we rolled down the window.

"I see that the oil light just came on. Let's see how much is left," Josh replied as we checked the oil. "Not much left, maybe a quart and a half," he replied as he raised the dipstick. "Amon lives right near here. Let me call him and see what he says," Josh said. He always seemed able to figure out the best thing to do.

Familiar with that section of town, Josh took the taxi to get some oil. Then, we took the van to Amon's house. He called a mechanic, who came after about an hour to diagnose the problem. The mechanic went to look for a new oil seal to replace the one that burst when the van started that morning. As we waited, we talked. I realized we had completely neglected our worship and prayer that morning. We forgot our need for God.

Late in the afternoon, the mechanic returned with the parts and made the repairs. We returned to the hotel hungry, tired, and frustrated. We had accomplished nothing on our list. Now we had to delay our departure until the following week. At least God in mercy spared the van from major engine damage. I felt grateful for that. However, I learned a big lesson: Remember to pray! Even when it seems we are too busy for anything else, remember to pray! We must be in a constant attitude of prayer throughout the day. Jesus even prayed the entire night through when He had a lot to do. I am thankful for God's patience with me. I am a slow student, but He still loves and forgives. This lesson I would not forget!

We enjoyed a safe and uneventful trip to Kendu Bay with the generator. The publishing house employees felt very grateful for the gift that would allow the press to continue operating. Now, eight years later, they still use that generator to power the printing press. We collected another large order of Swahili books while there and placed an order for the future.

Back at Kibidula, sand and bricks arrived daily at the building site of our new home in an effort to beat the approaching rainy season. I also made some headway on the delinquent accounting. Thankful for God's blessings, we finally knew constant prayer had become our only lifeline. "Pray without ceasing" (1 Thessalonians 5:17).

Chapter 7
GOD'S WORK EXPANDS

In our committee meetings, we frequently discussed the need to establish a school to train lay people to be self-supporting evangelists and to carry the gospel to unentered areas. We all agreed this school should include training in evangelism, agriculture, and village health. Jason Harral took the initiative to start the school.

In November, he told us that after finishing the church measuring for South-West Tanzania Field, he would focus all his energy on opening the Kibidula Training Center. Looking back, I realize that the opening of this training center became the most significant event in our years at Kibidula. Keith enrolled as one of the first students.

Unfortunately, many of our early letters to our daughter, Laura, got lost in the mail. How we longed to see her! In mid-December, she came for a visit during school break. When I saw her at the airport, I couldn't keep the tears of joy back. We had missed her so much.

When our family traveled to Ruaha National Park, we learned another lesson about living in Africa. Jared and several others rode on the top of our van as our guide helped us find lions. Under the guide's instruction, I drove to within twenty feet of six lions that lounged on a carpet of green grass. After a bit, I heard Jared say, "Open the window and let me in. I don't like the way that lion looks at me." When Jared shifted a bit on top of the van, one lioness noticed him. She stared at him intently as her tail twitched rapidly from side to side. Her legs and body looked tense as if she planned to spring.

"Start the engine and drive away!" ordered the guide. I didn't need any coaxing to quickly start the engine. As I drove off, Jared

scrambled into the van on the opposite side from the lions. The engine startled the lions, and they all jumped up and ran a short distance away. We learned a valuable lesson about staying inside of the vehicle. Obviously, Jared's angel continued to protect him.

The lion on the left threatened to attack Jared.

On the last day of the year, we staked out the corners of the new house. It overlooked one of the beautiful valleys at Kibidula, which reminded us of the Minnesota River Valley at Marybeth's childhood home. Purchasing building supplies consumed a lot of my time now as the foundation of the house took shape. Jared, my right-hand man on the site, gave me daily reports on the progress. His high energy level kept the building crew moving.

We were saddened when Rudy announced in mid-May that he and his family needed to return home permanently to care for Michelle's ailing father. Josh returned home also, and their previous responsibilities fell on my shoulders.

When Laura came for another visit in June, she brought with her a tall, quiet young man named Ben. Clearly, they enjoyed being together, and he had come to meet the family. They traveled with us to Mwanza. A major evangelistic meeting from Mwanza's Kirumba Stadium was televised and rebroadcast to sites all across Africa. Again, leaders asked us to help provide books for this event. Each day, the entire family sold books to the many visitors and members who attended the meetings.

Jared set out to be the top salesman. One day I overheard him trying to convince a young single man to buy an illustrated children's Bible. I felt confident that he could not possibly interest him in the book. "Look," Jared said, "someday you will get married and have children. Then, the children will grow up and learn to read. Then, you will need this Bible! You better buy it now while you can." He made the sale.

Due to the terrible shortage of books in Tanzania, our sales were brisk. Before the meetings, I felt impressed to buy seven thousand dollars' worth of Swahili Bibles for this event, a big investment for us. As the meetings neared their close, I wondered what I would do with all these Bibles. One day a leader of the Northwest Pacific Union (major sponsors of the event) approached me. "We hear you might have Bibles. We have searched the city and can't find any. We prayed earnestly to find Bibles for those who will be baptized."

"Yes, I purchased two thousand Bibles to sell," I replied. "Now I know why God impressed me to buy so many. Praise God, His love provided Bibles for the new members."

On the last Friday of the meetings, I started loading unsold books to take back on the train. They needed to reach the station by

3:00 P.M. Daudi Ndekeja, the Conference publishing director, literally stood in my way. "I will not let you take the books back. The colporteurs here are my children, and they hunger for more books. You must leave them behind."

Knowing that credit sales of books in Africa always meant a big loss, I regretfully responded, "Daudi, I cannot leave them here without you paying for them. You know that."

As I picked up a box of books to load into the van, he grabbed the other end of the box. Much younger and stronger than I, Daudi pulled one way, and I pulled the other as the box moved back and forth. I could also see that he was serious, even though we were laughing with each other. The deadline for shipping was fast approaching. But as fast as I loaded books, Daudi unloaded them.

A newly baptized girl smiles after receiving the gift of a new Bible.

Finally, in desperation, I said, "Daudi, you can keep all the books in this box on credit if you count them all and put them on a list over in that room." As he counted, I loaded boxes as fast as I could. As soon as he came out, I gave him another box. In twenty minutes, the van was loaded and on its way, but Daudi smiled as he walked away with food for his colporteurs.

The sweat poured off me as I worked furiously in Dar to "hurry up" the clearing of a container through customs. But bureaucracy is not easily hurried. Every day for four days, I had been told the container would come out, and now I had reached the limit of my patience. I felt ready to explode as I moved more boxes in our existing literature container to accommodate the hoped-for shipment.

Just at that moment, a tiny little lady appeared at the doorway of the container. She flashed me a big smile and asked in the sweetest voice, "Could I get some literature for the prisoners in the Dodoma prison?"

"Huh?" I replied as I wiped the sweat from my glasses to see who I was talking to. The big smile and sincerity of that little colporteur lady melted all my frustration on the spot. How could I be angry in the presence of one of God's workers?

That blessed meeting sparked a partnership between Amina Kikula and Kibidula. We began to sponsor her work in the prison by providing soap, toothbrushes, and toothpaste for prisoners. But that was just an opener for her real agenda—Bible studies. When I met Amina, she had 170 Bible studies going in the Dodoma prison. Periodically, she traveled there with a pastor to baptize prisoners. We provided Bibles, Swahili hymnals, and spiritual books for the prisoners. This contact with Amina Kikula sparked Kibidula to open libraries and provide books for many prisons and schools across Tanzania.

Amina told me about the reception she received when she first requested permission to enter the prison. They laughed her to scorn.

"What? You must be crazy! You're a woman. We don't let women into the prison! These men haven't even seen a woman in years. It is not safe at all!" However, they did not know the perseverance of this little colporteur or the mighty God that she served! She prayed and returned to the prison again and again, finally reaching high-level administrators in the prison system. Finally, the Lord honored her persistence, and she went where no other woman had gone—right in with the prisoners. She eventually ministered to the section reserved for those under condemnation of death. Six armed guards escorted her through the prison, but in my mind, I wonder how many angels were by her side. Nearly two hundred prisoners were baptized as a result of this work, and I praise God for divine appointments.

In October of 2002, I sold books at an evangelistic meeting conducted by Jason Harral in Mbeya. I noticed that each day, a young woman from the choir came to our sales booth and stared longingly at the Bibles. Sometimes, she would pick one up and caress it. I had never seen anyone handle a Bible like that before.

"What's your name?" I asked trying to strike up a conversation. "Would you like to buy a Bible?"

She looked down as tears formed in her eyes. "My name is Joyce," she replied. "I live with my widowed mother and younger brothers and sisters. I've never had a Bible, and I wish so much that I had the money to buy one."

I saw that she was telling the truth, and now the tears started to form in my eyes. "As of today, you have a Bible," I said as I handed it to her. As she took the Bible in her hands, she closed her eyes, held the Bible up to her lips, and kissed it. She thanked me profusely.

I felt a thrill go through my body to see her holding that Bible. Deeply moved, I wondered how many others longed to have Bibles but simply could not afford them. Soon after that I started a Bible fund at Kibidula. Through the generous donations of many people,

Barry with Amina Kikula, the brave colporteur whose prison ministry has resulted in more than two hundred baptisms.

we gave away more than three thousand five hundred Bibles over the years, mostly to newly baptized members. I thank God for sending Joyce to me because putting Bibles in the hands of new members is my most rewarding experience in Africa.

Amazingly, at the same meetings, a literature evangelist named Luvale kept coming by to handle the books at our booth. He would pick up each book in succession, look it over, and then set it down. After the third day of seeing this behavior, I asked the publishing director of the field why he didn't buy any books.

"He doesn't have any money to buy books," was the simple reply.

"How can you be a book salesman if you have no money to buy the books?" I asked incredulously. "How frustrating!"

"Unfortunately, many of our literature evangelists have no capital."

At the conclusion of the meetings, we gave fifty dollars' worth of books to twenty literature evangelists in Mbeya as a pilot program. Eventually, we gave free books as capital to more than one thousand literature evangelists across Tanzania. Luvale is still selling books today and is one of the assistant publishing directors in Mbeya.

This marked the beginning of a steady and rapid expansion of Kibidula's book ministry. Eventually, we had twenty-two bookstores across the country and during my years at Kibidula, we sold more than 425,000 books to colporteurs. God had truly blessed us since the early days of conflict in the publishing work. Each month as I prepared the sales records, I shouted for joy as I saw the thousands of soul-winning books placed in the hands of truth-seeking readers.

One last story emerged from those evangelistic meetings in Mbeya—the miracle of Helena Mwakalinga. At age fourteen, Helena had committed her life in the service of the Catholic Church as a nun. By 1999, she took her final vows to be faithful to the Catholic Church for the rest of her life. Happy in her commitment, she had no idea that God had other plans for her.

That same year of 1999, she suffered a health setback with a heart condition at only twenty-five years of age. She became very thin. Finally, they sent her by bus to a large hospital in Songea. According to God's providence, she sat next to an Adventist couple, who shared freely with her about something she had never heard of before—the Sabbath. As they traveled, the couple read Swahili tracts supplied by Kibidula. She eagerly read "over their shoulders" about this fascinating new teaching. This spawned a desire in her heart to become a Sabbath keeper. However, others in the convent chastised her until she finally lost her desire to pursue the matter.

Two years later, after another trip to the hospital, Helena returned to the convent and unlocked her suitcase. A book dropped

Helena holds the book that mysteriously appeared in her locked suitcase.

out. Amazed, she knew she kept her suitcase locked at all times on the trip, and the key had never left her presence. She inquired of others how this book could have gotten into her suitcase, but no one knew. The Swahili book was *Danieli na Siku Zetu* (*Daniel and Our Times*), a book sold by Kibidula. Because we know from the story of Peter in the Bible that angels have a special way with locks, we feel confident that an angel put the book into her suitcase.

Helena read the book carefully, and after studying the Scriptures, decided to leave the sisterhood in June 2002. In October, two of our Kibidula lay Bible workers met Helena as they did door-to-door work in preparation for evangelistic meetings. She attended the meetings and was baptized. She later attended our evangelism training school. Although her former leaders threatened her with death, she said, "I am following Jesus now, and I am not afraid. They cannot hurt me."

Who knows how many people have found the truth through publications? Helena lives as a testimony to the work of these silent messengers on the hearts of readers.

Chapter 8
THE MAMA'S HOUSE

After we had been at Kibidula for about six months, someone summoned Marybeth to the home of a woman having trouble giving birth. By the time she arrived at the home, the babies (yes, twins) had already been born. The conditions shocked Marybeth. As she entered the thatched-roof mud house, her eyes took a little time to become accustomed to the darkness. She saw the babies had been born on a small pile of straw. As she moved closer, she barely stifled a scream as a small animal scurried out of her path. A number of other guinea pigs frolicked in the straw.

She cringed again when she realized that the babies were wrapped in pieces of cloth that must have served as rugs on the dirt floor. Each baby's cord had been tied off with a dirty cloth about six inches from the baby's body. The other end was wrapped behind the baby's neck and tied to its left arm to satisfy a local superstition.

As time went on, she saw other things that made her heart ache for the horrible birth conditions the village women endured, including rats running through the room. However, she noticed no reaction from Cecelia, an Adventist village midwife who had become her teammate, and the other women in the room. She began to understand that to them such filthy conditions seemed normal. On another occasion, she wondered why the people took the time to paint vertical white stripes down their mud walls. However, when the chickens came in to roost that night, she found out that they were the artists who striped the walls with their droppings.

At first, she tried to get the women to the government hospital in Mafinga for birthing. However, she soon learned that the women feared to go there because too many women and children died there. (Conditions have improved since that time.) After taking one woman to town for delivery following a slow labor, Marybeth returned the next day and learned how the nurses had "hurried" the delivery. They tied a large cloth loosely around the abdomen of the pregnant woman. Then, they began to twist the cloth like a tourniquet around the woman's stomach. Tighter and tighter they squeezed until they forced the baby out. Marybeth found the baby crying a strange, shrill scream. The nurses had simply laid it aside to die. She immediately took the baby to a private hospital some distance away, where they saved the baby's life.

These experiences caused Marybeth to determine to provide help to the village women near Kibidula. Eventually, we built a little birthing room near our new home, equipped with running water, electricity, and two clean beds. We dubbed it the "mama's house," and the women began to come for help. Marybeth lacked modern equipment, so she made a partnership with God. *Dear Lord,* she prayed, *help me to do my best when people come for help. I will depend on You, the Great Physician, to do Your work.* God blessed her faith.

We got used to the unpredictable schedule of a midwife. She could be called upon any time of the day or night. For night travel, I drove the van. Frequently our faithful workers Jonas and Mika acted as messengers and guides.

Life in a rural village can be boring, so the birth of a new baby becomes an exciting event. Often, by the time we reached the home with our old van, a crowd had gathered. All the grandmas and aunties and sisters wanted to watch the birth. We set a limit of two attendants to accompany the expectant mother to the "mama's house," but seldom could enforce it. I would ask, "Marybeth, didn't we say only two could accompany the mother? I count at least five in there. How many do you count?"

Marybeth, April, and Andrew with the parents of a newly delivered baby girl.

Marybeth would reply, "Barry, you'll have to fight them to get them out. This mother's labor pains keep coming faster. Just block the door before more visitors get in!"

One time, after a prolonged labor, Marybeth checked to see if the baby's head was coming out. Shocked, she saw a patch of white hair on the top of the baby's head. She wondered what she had done wrong! But she had little time to wonder, for the shoulders were stuck. She did a couple of quick maneuvers, and a tiny albino baby was born!

When we returned from a three-month furlough, we heard reports of the number of babies that died during home births or in the hospital while Marybeth was gone. The law required firstborn children and those of older women to be delivered at the hospital. However, since no babies had died at the "mama's house," the village women would intentionally arrive at the last minute, hoping Marybeth would deliver them herself. One day, Marybeth was confronted with a birth in which the cord had come out before the baby. "Help me, God," she pleaded, knowing the urgency of the situation.

The mother needed a C-section, but no surgeon was available. The only thing to do was to get that baby out as fast as possible. After delivery, she tried everything to resuscitate the unresponsive baby—CPR, vigorous rubbing, resuscitator bag, and, most important, urgent prayer. Nothing worked, and the minutes slipped by. Marybeth started dipping the baby into buckets of hot and cold water, alternating between the two. Dipping, praying, dipping, praying. Finally, the baby's eyes opened slightly, and the baby breathed in its first breath. Praise God! Another life was saved. By the next morning, the baby appeared strong and healthy. Marybeth smiled a big smile of gratitude to God as she drove the mother home. God is good!

Altogether, Marybeth delivered about one hundred fifty babies. But she also provided treatment for many other problems. Kind friends gave her "helping people" money to enable her to get necessary treatment for needy cases. A woman came whose bladder had leaked for nine years. Her husband had left her, and no one would come near her because she reeked of urine all the time. Marybeth arranged repair surgery for her. Another woman's uterus had been coming out for ten years. It is a wonder that she didn't die from infection, for she continually just poked it back inside. Marybeth helped her get the surgery she desperately needed. Another woman, anemic after fifteen years of almost continual bleeding, rejoiced when Marybeth got help for her. All these women expressed gratitude to be healthy again, and they appreciatively read the religious literature that Marybeth gave out. The villagers grew to love her dearly. She has become my hero as well, teaching me how to love people as Jesus did.

Other emergencies also came along. We saw a young girl fall while running in the village. Her upper lip was nearly severed by her teeth. Because it was Saturday, she knew no emergency-room doctor was on duty at the hospital. Although Marybeth had never before done stitches, she ran for her medical bag in the car and stitched the lip while sitting on the ground next to a cornfield. The lip healed well.

One more story will illustrate the need and tragedy that occur daily.

Debora Kibiki gazed out the door of their mud hut as the lightly falling rain signaled the end of the six-month dry season. Even though she ranked as the top student in her class in Matanana school, she would be expected to help the family plant the new crop of corn. Little brother Tumaini slept on her back in a sling while her parents and other siblings waited for the rain to subside.

Suddenly their peace was shattered as lightning struck the thatched roof and electrified the house. The force of the strike threw Debora and Tumaini out the door. Shrieks of terror filled the air as the rest of the family sought to escape the blazing home. Regaining their senses, they realized that eleven-year-old Debora was not breathing. Not knowing what to do, they sent someone by bicycle to fetch Marybeth.

Because I had taken our vehicle to evaluate a nearby village for evangelistic meetings, Marybeth had to search for a vehicle to borrow. By the time she arrived at the house where the tragedy happened, nearly half an hour had passed. Marybeth was confused as the family kept telling her that the girl had been burned.

She showed no vital signs. Loading Debora's body and the family into the pickup, they drove to the "mama's house" near our home. Finally, someone mentioned the word *lightning,* and Marybeth understood that the girl had probably died instantly from the lightning strike. By God's mercy, little Tumaini still lived, although the side of his head that lay against his sister at the time of the strike was badly burned.

I arrived with our vehicle about the time my wife understood the cause of Debora's death. As I stared in stunned disbelief at Debora's body, Marybeth let out a shout of hope, "He's nursing!" Sure enough, the mother had offered her breast to little Tumaini, and he nursed with vigor. We quickly loaded him and his parents into the Land Cruiser, and I raced them to the hospital thirty minutes away.

As I drove, my mind whirled, trying to comprehend this latest tragedy. *With AIDS and malaria and other diseases reaping their daily toll, these poor villagers seem accustomed to tragedy. Satan's scepter of death continually stalks the land. But how could this happen to an innocent young girl?* How easy it would be to despair. However, as I drove, the Lord reminded me of the meaning of little Tumaini's Swahili name—"hope." In spite of tragedy, Hope still lived. Yes, because of Jesus, hope was still alive! Praise God for hope! At all costs we must keep Christian hope alive. (And Baby Hope is still alive today.)

Through God's grace, Marybeth has brought life and hope into the lives of many people. That is our work. Jesus ministered to people day by day while on this earth. God gives us a variety of skills and talents to also use in ministry. We can find true satisfaction only in using those skills and talents in doing the work God assigns us.

Is God calling you to touch people's lives for Him?

Chapter 9
COURAGE AND SACRIFICE

Most of the graduates of our evangelism training program were hired at the completion of their training. Local conferences hired some. Others, sponsored by their local churches, worked in unentered areas. We hired many because Kibidula's missionary program expanded rapidly under the Lord's blessing from four to thirty lay missionaries. Some were sponsored by Sabbath School classes, churches, and individuals in first-world countries. We provided them with tools for their work, such as bicycles, Swahili Bible studies and tracts, Bibles and a reference library of books, along with small portable horn speaker systems. When they returned twice a year to give reports and make plans, we would offer refresher courses and clothing for their families.

However, their work faced severe challenges. The stipends were modest, especially for large families. They often faced stiff opposition to their labor. Most of their stories of courage, faith, sacrifice, and persistence go unnoticed except in the books of heaven. I must share two of them.

When I asked Pastor Joshua Kajula, the president of South-West Tanzania Field to give me the name of an unentered area that was in desperate need, he said, "Brother Mosier, a big valley on the other side of Iringa is completely unentered. The people are mostly Muslim, so the work will be very tough, but we wish you could place someone in the village of Mahenge in that valley." As the lay missionary and evangelism coordinator for Kibidula, I constantly sought new areas to place workers.

Knowing that we needed a strong person to go to that valley, I

called Paulo Joseph, a graduate of Kibidula Training Center. He moved there almost immediately with his wife and three children. Arriving on a Thursday evening, Paulo and family moved into the house he had arranged to rent on his scouting trip. The sweat beaded on their foreheads as they moved their modest belongings into the three-room mud hut with a metal roof. This hot, desert area received very little rainfall, and the local people were very poor. The Joseph family knelt in prayer before sleeping for the night, asking that God would help them to reach the people of this village.

The next morning, Friday, he sent his three children to fetch water from the nearby Ruaha River for their Sabbath preparations. The oldest, twenty-one, was an adopted son whom he had converted. Fourteen-year-old Jose and

Stephano Kasiri, my trusted book distribution worker, along with the Vinsons and April preparing a shipment of books for the free colporteur capital program.

eleven-year-old Tina followed him. The boys were excited about helping their father to share the gospel.

Arriving at the river, they were intrigued by the many birds. They watched village women and children going into the shallows to fill their water pails, and when the others had left, they took their turn. Not familiar with rivers of this size, they entered timidly. After filling the first and second pails, the older boy decided to go out a bit farther to cool his legs on this hot morning before filling the third pail. At that location, the river curved, forming a large eddy just beyond the shallows.

Suddenly, the older boy's feet slipped out from under him. Immediately, he was caught in the circling waters of the eddy. He had no idea how to swim and started thrashing his arms in panic. "Jose! Help me!" he screamed.

Jose looked in terror as his brother's head disappeared beneath the muddy water again. "I'm coming!" he shouted as he raced toward the river. His loyal heart could not watch his brother drown while there was strength left in his own body. He would save his brother! Leaping into the deep water, he inhaled water and started choking and sputtering. He kicked desperately for any kind of foothold, but had never been in water over his head before and didn't know how to swim. Now, both boys thrashed about in panic, trying to reach the shore. The circling eddy confused them and kept them from reaching the safety of the bank.

Finally, Tina could watch no longer and jumped in too. Now all three faced drowning. As their lungs filled with water, their thrashing subsided, and they slipped into unconsciousness. A Muslim man downstream saw a body floating by. He quickly pulled Tina out of the river. Fortunately, she was still alive and revived. Eventually, she was able to speak, and told the man about her brothers. Quickly the villagers began to look for them, but it was too late. They took Tina home to tell her parents the heartbreaking story.

The parents raced to the river, but found nothing but the two buckets of water remaining on the bank. Others joined them as they raced along the river for any evidence of their sons, but could find none.

By the time word reached us that night at Kibidula, the story didn't make much sense. However, Jason Fournier and I headed for Mahenge. We arrived at 2:00 A.M. and from outside the house we could hear the wailing from the grief-stricken parents. After expressing our sorrow and sympathy, we sat on the mud floor as the house filled with mourners. A steady stream of people came and went, but none of us knew what to say or do. I felt the warm tears course down my cheeks as I thought of my own two sons. How could this tragedy happen? Why? Why?

An Adventist church about thirty kilometers away sent some of their choir, and they sang hymns of faith and comfort. From time to time, family members would shout out their frustrations and wail loudly in the African way of mourning. The choir's beautiful harmony soothed my heart as I leaned against the mud wall shooing the occasional mosquitoes that buzzed about.

I could not bring myself to ask Paulo the obvious question: What would he do now? Besides, I knew what the answer had to be. Without a doubt, he would return home and try never again to hear the name of this place where the tragedy happened.

In the morning, a group of village men gathered at Paulo's home. After they left, Jason told me that they had gone to search for the body of the older boy in the river. They had recovered Jose's body later on the day of the accident. This time, they failed. Not long after that, Paulo approached me. He looked me straight in the eye, set his jaw, and said in very broken English, "*Mosier.* You think I go home now?" There was a pause as he gathered his courage. "After

F. — 3

Paulo Joseph (second from left) with his wife and daughter at the site where their two sons had drowned two years before.

five graves here, then my work will finish this village. I stay missionary here."

It took me a moment to grasp what Paulo meant. He refused to leave Mahenge until either his entire family was buried here or the work was finished. I was speechless as I contemplated the courage and faith of this family in the face of tragedy.

"*Mungu akubariki* [May God bless you], Paulo," I replied.

After the doctor from Iringa came to examine the body at noon, the burial service was ready to commence. Paulo led me by the arm into the bedroom. There on the bed lay Jose's body wrapped in a white sheet. "You take picture Jose for me last time?" he asked. As he folded back the sheet and I looked at the beautiful face of his dead son, I thought of Jared and the tractor accident. I thought of my sons helping me in my work and the horrible loss that Paulo and his family suffered. Then I couldn't hold back my tears any longer. I started to weep uncontrollably. Paulo and I wrapped our arms around each others' shoulders as we let the tears fall freely. We sobbed there for some time before I managed to take the picture. Then we proceeded to the grave site.

This drowning of the two boys became big news in a village of only a thousand people. Paulo's name was a household word now. People gathered in mass at the funeral to see what would happen. Surely, this stranger would move away after this tragedy. They listened and waited.

Then, Paulo started to speak, "My family and I came to bring the gospel to this village. I am not going to leave until there are five graves here from my family. I am inviting anyone here who would like to study the Bible to let me know so we can begin."

I don't remember what else he said. His remarks were brief. I could only stand in awe of the courage and faith of this missionary family. I wondered whether I would have had this kind of courage under similar circumstances.

When I stopped again after a month to check on Paulo, he told me about the evangelistic meetings in progress. Then, after another month, I came back on a Sabbath for the baptism of the first ten converts in Mahenge. On the way back from the river, Paulo approached me again, "*Mosier,* the river that take away my two children, now give me ten new children."

God gives us strength to meet the trials that come our way. He helps us prepare our characters to stand in the last days. Let us each meet our trials with courage and faith as we trust the Lord with all our hearts. I long to see the sweet, sweet reunion in heaven when Paulo and his sons are reunited. "We know that all things work together for good to them that love God, to them who are the called according to his purpose" (Romans 8:28).

Joseph Kyando was another of our lay missionaries. He stood about five feet four inches tall and had a powerful build with broad shoulders and a thick neck. He loved to sing and had a deep bass voice. Joseph, slightly cross-eyed, had experienced an accident years before that damaged his knee and left a perpetual limp.

He trained as a clinical officer and was looked upon as a doctor by all who knew him. We never knew what he would do or say next, as he reveled in doing the unpredictable. I remember Jason Harral wanting to drag him off the stage during his health talk in Mbeya when he announced that AIDS could be cured with lemons!

But he willingly worked in the toughest areas. When I hired him as a Kibidula lay missionary following his graduation, we called him to work in Rukwa Valley. The people of the valley faced problems of immorality, alcoholism, and laziness. Hot and infested with malaria, this area was inaccessible during the rainy season. Although it included hundreds of villages, Rukwa was virtually untouched with the gospel message.

I did not know about the plans Joseph had already made with Pastor Mtenzi in the field office. His goal with God: to open fifteen new companies of believers and build fifteen new churches in Rukwa Valley within five years. I'm glad that I didn't know about his goal, or I would have urged him to be more realistic.

Joseph, a natural leader, received a special gift from God—the ability to inspire others to help him with his work. That gift touched both Keith and me too. Each year Joseph returned with thrilling reports of how the work was progressing. Each year I would give him funds to build more churches. Keith went to the valley in 2003 to help do two evangelistic meetings and build three churches. He inspired half a dozen people to help with the work, placing them in strategic villages throughout the valley. In fact, some of our most successful lay missionaries through the years were people that Joseph originally called and trained.

Each year he pleaded with me for a motorcycle to help him oversee the work. Finally, one day as I saw him limping along, I realized that his request was valid, and we purchased a motorcycle for him. His persistence and contagious enthusiasm had worked again! Although his wife refused to live in Rukwa, he visited her periodically at their home in Mbeya.

When Pastor Mtenzi joined our staff in 2006 as the new evangelism and lay missionary coordinator, he agreed to team up with Joseph in doing several evangelistic series and building several churches in July 2006.

Coordinating a large team, they managed to do five evangelistic series and construct five churches over a period of only six weeks. On August 5, they rejoiced to complete the construction of Ilambo church, the fifteenth church in the valley and the seventeenth company of believers organized since Joseph had started the work in 2001. They were thrilled that the Lord had answered their prayers in meeting the original goals.

On August 29, 2006, my family and I landed in Dar, returning from our furlough. After every trip to America, we face a short readjustment period as we try to adapt from the first world to the sights, sounds, and smells of the third world again. As I drove past the dirty little stores that lined Nyerere Road, my cell phone rang. I heard the familiar voice of Pastor Mtenzi on the line. "Mosier, I am calling to tell you that Joseph Kyando died yesterday. Can you come to the funeral?" I could hardly believe my ears.

Yet, it was true. On August 27, Joseph became very ill with malaria. They transported him from the hospital in Sumbawanga, where his wife came to be with him. He died the next day. His last words to his wife were, "I thank God for letting me finish what we planned. You see, He has allowed me to finish the work and now permitted this disease to take my life."

I wept as I thought of this sudden death of my friend Joseph Kyando. Yet as I considered his last words, I could see he had no regrets. He had persevered in his work and achieved the goal of soul winning that he had set together with the Lord. God inspired him to set these exact goals and enabled him to achieve them. I look forward to meeting Joseph in heaven. Then, I will once again hear his rich bass voice ring forth as the Rukwa choir sings praises to God for His unfathomable love.

What kind of risks do you and I take for Jesus each day? Are we facing our opportunities with courage and perseverance? I hope that when we meet our neighbors on the street, we willingly risk our friendship by telling what Jesus means to us or invite them to a Bible study or to evangelistic meetings. When I contemplate the labors of Paulo and Joseph, I am inspired to do more for Jesus. I know of many more dedicated people of courage, faith, sacrifice, and perseverance, but these two are enough to remind me of the supreme sacrifice of Jesus for me. In these last days, as each of us stands on the front lines of the great controversy, may we be willing to take risks for Jesus as we enjoy the work that really satisfies under the guidance from the Holy Spirit.

Chapter 10
KINDNESS IS NEVER WASTED

While visiting my good friend Pastor Kajula in his office one day, we discussed our lay missionaries and the challenges we faced. "Brother Mosier, there is one village that has had several evangelistic series, but we have never been able to establish a church there. I wonder if you could help us to start a work in the Muslim village of Kananga?"* he asked. We knelt in his office and left it in God's hands to open the way.

I wrote to my friends Keith and Barb Christiansen in Wisconsin about the problem. They agreed to come in May of the following year to hold evangelistic meetings and build a church—a project similar to one previously done in Mahenge. We called two of our evangelism school graduates, Daudi Simzosha and Grace Njako, to do Bible work in Kananga for five months in preparation for the meetings.

Later, when Reuben and I drove to Kananga, Daudi gave us his report. "We contacted three Muslim groups in this town," he explained. "One of them is very *kali* [fierce], but the other two are not so strict. Their people do not really know much about the Muslim faith; many pagan beliefs are still prevalent. The other Christian group in town keeps a large herd of pigs that is very offensive to the Muslims." I couldn't imagine why they made such a blunder in a Muslim community.

"Have you acquired a plot on which to build a church yet?" I asked.

"Yes, but it will be expensive compared to other places. They want two hundred fifty dollars for it. We now study with twelve

*Not the real name of the village.

Reuben Kingagam-kono, our translator, along with Barb and Keith Christiansen, who held the meetings in the Muslim village of Kananga.

people, but we find it hard to get studies here. The leaders follow us around. After we leave, they visit and threaten to curse the people with witchcraft. After that, the study is usually over," he answered.

As we left I saw a picture prominently displayed in one of the nearby shops. I inquired who was in the picture, although I recognized the face immediately. "That is Osama bin Laden, the ruler of the world," the shopkeeper replied. I thought, *We need to pray more.*

I felt bad for Daudi when I visited his home. He and his brave wife, Telezia, had moved into three little rooms in a low-end apartment with their six children. One of the boys suffered from a heart problem that was compounded by the heat. Yet they smiled and seemed to be in good spirits. As I left extra money with them for food and doctor bills, I acknowledged that my own life was pretty soft in comparison. Two weeks later, our church building team arrived in Kananga to build a new church.

When Keith and Barb arrived at our home with their daughter Ceri, we gave them a couple of days to rest while we packed things to take to Kananga. Barb helped Marybeth care for Happy, the little AIDS baby who lived with us. "Barry, I don't know how I will be able to travel to Kananga with Happy tomorrow," said Marybeth wearily. "She is not very strong."

"I know," I replied. "Let's leave it in the Lord's hands. He will show us what to do."

Happy had come to us after her mother died of AIDS. The father had died sometime earlier. Doris and Jean Luc Waber, our kindhearted neighbors from across the valley, had started helping the older children, and little Happy went to live with Godfrey Sanga. One Sabbath morning at church, Godfrey's wife handed Happy to Marybeth and said, "We don't know what to do with her. She is always sick and can't keep any food down." Marybeth never said No to someone in need. She took the skeleton of a girl in her arms, and we had a new family member.

At home, Marybeth weighed the little one-and-a-half-year-old baby and found that she weighed seven pounds, ten ounces. Her arms and legs looked like toothpicks and her ribs stuck out. No one had ever seen her smile. She was not even strong enough to turn over. We decided to care for her, but our goals seemed simple. We wanted her to experience love in her life. Maybe then she would smile. A smile seemed like a big assignment at first as her big eyes followed her white-skinned caregivers around the room with terror. However, as time went on, she grew to trust us.

Her care demanded Marybeth give her fever-reducing medicine every four hours around the clock in order for her to keep any food

Happy, the AIDS orphan who lived with us for ten months before her death.

down. She also needed treatment for her tuberculosis. I worried about Marybeth's health as she cared for Happy, but she brushed aside my concerns.

After nine months, Happy could sit up and play with toys, but best of all, she could laugh! She loved to eat spaghetti and bananas. Marybeth loved her dearly and prayed earnestly for the Lord to heal her. However, this time of joy was short. The month before Keith and Barb arrived, Happy's health took another nosedive.

On the morning we were to leave for Kananga, Marybeth rocked Happy in our living room while I studied my Bible. Quietly, Marybeth whispered, "I think Happy has stopped breathing. She's gone."

We buried her later that day with many tears, but no regrets. The villagers looked on in amazement to watch white people crying for a black baby. Thanks to Marybeth, the baby had known great love, and she had smiled. We hope to see her in the resurrection with a new healthy body. "Inasmuch as ye have done it unto one of the least of these my brethren, ye have done it unto me" (Matthew 25:40). Although I am a selfish person by nature, I thanked God who gave me Marybeth to teach me more about unselfish love.

The next day we drove to Kananga to start the meetings. The police and local officials allowed us to use the government meeting area. We were exited and thrilled when a thousand people attended the opening meeting on Friday evening. Barb gave a fascinating health talk, weaving in passages from the Koran. Then Keith gave a solid presentation from the Scriptures. Of course, our horn speakers blared out the message, even to distant areas of the town, with the help of our generator.

That night in our two-dollar-per-night hotel, we were awakened from our sleep early. Marybeth asked, "What is that eerie sound? It sounds like marching and chanting just outside the hotel."

"I don't know, but I don't like the sound of it," I answered.

The morning brought the answers to our questions. The mosque next door was buzzing with activity. A circle of men gathered at the mosque shouted a rhythmic chant as they marched in rotation— first one way, then the other. Further investigation revealed that this was the regional celebration for the birthday of Muhammad—the largest Muslim celebration of the year.

I shook my head in disbelief. How could I have made such a blunder? We could not begin evangelistic meetings in a Muslim community on the biggest Muslim holiday of the year. Since the Iraq war was on, Americans were not popular. We prayed earnestly for God to show us how to handle the situation.

Barb trusted that I would not bring them to a dangerous situation.

She walked around town to see the sights. Immediately children began to follow her. She soon led a crowd of children like a pied piper. She took pictures freely—especially of the children.

Later that day, shortly before our second meeting was to begin, the axe started to fall. A Muslim leader approached me in anger, "We thought that you were just going to get up and talk, but you conduct your meetings in a very evangelistic way." He confronted me near the meeting area.

"That's the only way we know how to do it." I could think not think of a better answer at the time.

"Besides that," he continued, getting hotter all the time, "your people took pictures of our sacred ceremonies today. Why? And what will you do with those pictures?"

"I'm sorry," I replied. "A lady at the mosque asked us to take her picture while she was cooking, so we did. We will erase it from our camera."

"Listen," he said, "if you want to know what you can do in this town, ask a man, not a woman!" Then, as if to silence me completely and reaching the height of his speech, he said, "Tomorrow we will celebrate the birth of Muhammad here on this government field. Get all of your things off of this field before then!"

Not an argumentative person, I wilted before this last blast. Only the Holy Spirit could have brought the following words from my lips: "We'll gladly remove our things, but is there anything we can do to help you celebrate the birthday of Muhammad?"

He looked at me dumbfounded. Clearly astonished at this question, he hesitated before he replied, "What about those horn speakers? Could we use them?" Anyone who has been in a Muslim city at 5:00 A.M. knows how Muslims use public-address systems to call the faithful to morning prayers.

"Sure," I replied, "but I will have to be there to operate them.

Maybe you could use the benches too if I left them on the field?"

He readily agreed, and we proceeded with our evening meeting. Shortly before we showed a section of the Jesus video, I saw two men dragging a woman away as she desperately shouted, "*Nataka kuona video tu!* [I just want to see the video!]" Looking out over the sizable crowd viewing the video, I understood that Kananga was a man's world.

The next morning we arrived early at the field to raise the speakers ten feet higher and set up our generator and sound system. People from the entire area had gathered to enjoy the celebration. A large crowd filled the field, and about eight Muslim leaders gathered on the stage. As they talked to the people, the most amazing words came from their mouths. "These *Wasabato* [Seventh-day Adventists] seem different. These good people let us use their speakers today. We work together. We travel the same path."

I could hardly believe my ears as leader after leader affirmed these kind words. Two things became immediately clear to me. One, in effect, they gave their people permission to attend our meetings. Second, by using our speakers themselves, they could hardly complain about our using them throughout our meetings.

"Be ye kind one to another" (Ephesians 4:32). "A soft answer turneth away wrath" (Proverbs 15:1). These Bible texts ran through my mind as I thought of what could have happened if I had fought back using unkind words against his verbal assault.

Our meetings progressed well with a steady attendance night by night. However, after a week, I needed to leave Kananga to attend meetings of the East-Central Africa Division in Kigali. The two-and-a-half-day journey included fourteen hours by bus and two airplane flights. Nervous about leaving the team for a week, I promised them that I would return for the baptism on the final Sabbath.

Now I needed to focus my thoughts on preparation for these

Baptism following the meetings at Kananga.

Division meetings. I needed help from God to assemble and present the requirements and rules for the ASI bicycle program that the Division would administer. God answered my need through the help of Noah Musema, the Division vice president, who managed to accomplish that task as he prepared to receive the requests from the ten different unions in their territory.

Leaving the Division meetings a day early, I raced back to Kananga in order to be able to attend the baptism. I wondered how the baptism would go in that Muslim community. I hoped there would not be a violent reaction. I managed to reach Kananga just as the very first church service in the new church building finished on Sabbath morning. As I approached the door, people began filing out of the service.

Stunned, I saw the regional Muslim imam and several local Muslim leaders leave the building. Was it really possible that they worshiped with us?

As I greeted my family, April poured out the latest news in a torrent of words. The meetings had progressed under God's guidance. Twenty-three new believers chose to be baptized, including eleven Muslims. Our Bible workers had invited the Muslim imam and other leaders to attend the service, and they had graciously accepted. We beamed with joy as we watched these new believers descend one by one into the water before a large crowd to signify their new lives in Jesus. Just as God's angels hold back the winds of strife, they held back any public outcry against us that day.

One of those baptized was a single mother of twins. We helped her as she struggled to keep her babies alive. Although one of them had lost sight in one eye due to vitamin A deficiency, the twins looked much better than when we first saw them.

That evening, Reuben held a special service before the meeting. Most of the people wore strings of devil charms as a means of protection from evil spirits. In fact, the imams in that area used witchcraft extensively to keep control of their people. Reuben explained the satanic evils of witchcraft and then demanded that all witches within hearing distance come forward to meet him. Our village missionary Daudi saw at least one known witch flee in terror from the meeting. Not one dared to come forward. Then, Reuben called for people to come and burn their charms, trusting in the power of Jesus. A number of people added their charms to the cleansing fire.

Then, Reuben called the regional imam forward to receive a Bible. He graciously accepted the Bible and Reuben asked him to address the crowd. In my mind I asked, *Reuben! What are you doing? Now, he might denounce our meetings.* However, God had planned all this.

As the imam addressed the crowd and those who had just received baptism, I remembered the Bible story of Balaam, when God put His own words into the prophet's mouth. Was this happening again before our very eyes as we listened in amazement to the imam's words? He said, "This preacher taught the Bible before you clearly for two weeks. If you didn't understand him, it's your own fault! Some of you chose baptism today. If that is your decision, stand by your new faith. Don't go back in your former beliefs." Our new church members cheered as they heard these amazing words of blessing from this Muslim imam.

The next morning as we packed up the car and trailer, Pastor Kajula happened by on his way back to Mbeya. Because of our overcrowded vehicles, he agreed to take Jared and Ceri back with him in his car. He said, "You know, I wondered if you would be leaving here with rocks on your back. Instead, by God's overwhelming grace, you leave with words of blessing. It seems too good to be true. I can hardly believe it, but I know now God's work will stand in this area. Praise His name."

As we returned home that day, I pondered two things. One, an act of kindness is never wasted. Second, in spite of our human blunders and mistakes, when it is God's work and His timing, a project cannot fail. God's answer to Paul in 2 Corinthians 12:9 remains forever true. "My strength is made perfect in weakness." Trusting in God, we can move forward with confidence as we seek daily to do His will.

Chap'

ANDREW JOINS THE FAMILY

Rosa leaned on her hoe as she bent again to plant another row of corn. Though only midmorning, already the heat of this late November day seemed oppressive. *When it gets this hot,* she thought, *we'll experience heavy rain in Kisada this afternoon.* She concluded she must work hard that day, because the next day the fields might be muddy. Rosa groaned as the baby inside her stretched again as if to say, "Nine months is enough. I want out!"

This tenth baby seemed harder than the first nine. Eight years had transpired since she had given birth to her previous child. Fortunately, only five children remained at home. Rosa acted as the main provider for her family; but her only source of income came from what these three acres of land produced. The crop they produced stood between her and starvation. Oh, how she wished that her husband, Matias, did not drink so much *ulanzi* (local beer). Hopelessly addicted, he got into frequent quarrels and fights when drunk. The family suffered because of his unpredictable behavior when drunk and their fear of violence. Usually a joker, his friends found him lots of fun when sober. His second wife, Anyes, enjoyed her beer also. That left most of the farming for Rosa. Anyes's six children only added to the work. This caused much friction between the two sides of the family.

By midday Rosa felt exhausted and started walking home. As she neared the familiar grass thatch of her hut, she longed for a rest, but knew that she needed to cook lunch quickly. In the afternoon she rested a little, but evening brought a familiar pain in her abdomen. In a few minutes, she knew the labor pains were beginning. She couldn't go to the nearby hospital because they had scolded her severely for getting pregnant again. They warned her that it would be most dangerous to get pregnant at her age, but it happened again anyway. What could she do? She preferred to deliver the baby at home, like the births of her other children, rather than risk the angry words of the nurses at the hospital again.

Two relatives came to attend her that evening as the pains came more frequently. At ten o'clock that night, the cry of her new little boy pierced the night and Rosa smiled wearily. As she lay on the mud floor of their hut, holding little Andreas Matias Kalinga in her arms, she became concerned as the bleeding continued. Three hours later, she slipped into unconsciousness. Soon she joined the one in sixteen women in Tanzania who die during childbirth.

The family became grief stricken at the loss of their faithful mother; wailing commenced immediately. The relatives glanced at each other, wondering what would happen to this newborn son. In the village, losing one's mother at birth is a death sentence because no one will nurse someone else's baby for fear of AIDS. Anyes made sure that everyone knew she did not want to raise another baby.

When our Kibidula team returned from a staff retreat, Anita Riederer's worker told her about the motherless infant. When she and Unity Temboh went to see the family to inquire how they could help, they found that the baby had not yet eaten three days after birth. As they asked the father what he intended to do, he handed the baby to Anita with a look of bewilderment on his face. His first wife had died. Soon his son would follow. Maybe these people could help.

By Friday, Anita and her little daughter Helena were becoming very bonded to the baby. They obviously faced a decision. Not ready to add to the family permanently, they brought the baby to Marybeth. The very next day, Matias came to church to find out about his son. With Watson Kiwovele helping us to translate, we gave him three options.

We offered to buy milk for the baby so they could feed him at their home. We hoped they wouldn't choose this option, as nonsterile techniques with a bottle usually lead to diarrhea and death. The second option was that we would pay for the baby to stay in the Lutheran orphanage in Mafinga. Finally, if the father would be willing to sign off on all the legal rights, we would adopt him and raise him as our own son. We gave Matias a month to decide which option to choose.

During that month, Marybeth grew to love Andreas as one of her own. At the end of the month, Matias gave us his answer, "If it wasn't for you people, the baby would be dead. I will sign the papers and you can raise him."

This legal adoption concept seemed hard for Tanzanians to understand. People are constantly taking their children to live with relatives. Maybe they are too poor to feed the child, or maybe the relative has money, and they think their child will get a better education. According to African culture, they find they cannot say No to this extended family as the ties to each other are so close. In fact, a father's younger brother would not be called an uncle, but *Baba Mdogo* (small father). Sometimes, the "loaned" child may act the part of a servant to earn his food and lodging. In any case, even some of our own staff asked us when we would give the child back to Matias. We had difficulty explaining that the child would become *our* child and would remain with us forever.

A month later, Matias came again to visit us. Thanking us again for giving Andreas the chance to live, he gave us a chicken he brought as a gift. "I am not able to pay for all that you spend for his food, but maybe this will help," he offered. Deeply touched by his thankfulness and sincerity, we accepted the chicken.

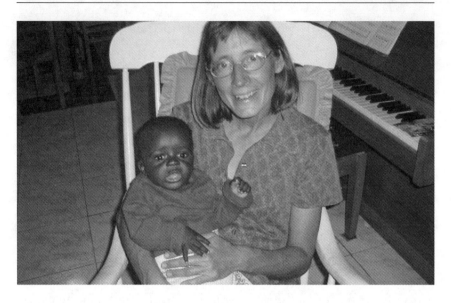

Marybeth with our adopted son, Andrew.

We decided to change the baby's name from Andreas Matias to Andrew Matthew. Then we started the legal process of adoption. We found out quickly in Tanzania, adoption is not a simple procedure. Only about thirty legal adoptions take place each year in the entire country. The government required us to go to the high court in Dar to facilitate the proceedings. Also the law stated that Andrew must live with us for three months before we could start the process. We had only two months to complete the adoption before our scheduled trip to America in late May.

Mr. Lukwaro, the lawyer who helped us, did wonders, and the Lord made everything work out. We left on furlough for America with a new son. A year later, we visited with a woman attorney in Dar who specialized in adoptions by foreigners. We explained how we did the court adoption in two months. She said, "That is impossible. It takes at least a year to a year and a half to do it. Show me your papers."

As we showed her the adoption certificate and all the legal papers, she just shook her head. "I handle most of the adoptions in Tanzania. All your papers are correct. What you did seems impossible in that short of a time."

"We serve a mighty God," was all we could reply.

God works in mysterious ways.

Chapter 12
MARTYR'S BLOOD IS STILL SEED

A hornbill flitted from one baobab tree to another as Amos Lulandala trudged across the hard-baked earth to another house, seeking people who wanted to study the Bible. He wondered when there would be a break in this unbearable heat as he detoured around one of the many thorn bushes in this area.

Paulo Joseph, our missionary in nearby Mahenge, had asked Amos to come to Tupendane as a self-supporting missionary. Amos accepted the call and moved with his wife and three children into a little two-room grass-roofed adobe hut in the village. The name *Tupendane* means "let's love each other," but that had definitely not been the history of this area. Years before, the Muslim slave traders had assembled their slaves in this hot, dry valley before marching them the three hundred miles to Bagamoyo on the coast for export.

The only thing that remains from those cruel days, amazingly, is the Muslim religion. About 80 percent of the inhabitants of the little village of five hundred people are Muslims. A few Christians live in the village, and in the surrounding countryside live the Maasai tribe. The Maasai are cattle herders who have clung to their traditional ways more than any other tribe in Tanzania. A proud people, they have resisted the Christian or Muslim religions and shunned education for their children. Traditionally, they live a nomadic life, as they seek grasslands to pasture their cattle and sheep.

As Amos tried to start a new congregation in Tupendane, he faced a big challenge. But he experienced a happy surprise when his first Bible study request came from a young Maasai girl who lived on the outskirts of the village with her family. Kulwa was seventeen years old, the oldest of twins. Her name in Swahili means "the first-born twin." She had accepted the three angels' messages with all her heart and looked forward to worshiping under the big baobab tree behind Amos's house each Sabbath morning. The pastor rarely visited this remote area, but she longed with eagerness for the day of her baptism.

Her stepfather, vehemently angry, insisted that she herd the cattle and sheep on Sabbath. He steadily sold the family's sheep for beer, and Kulwa had challenged him about it. Now, he decided to make this new religion a means of getting even. When she refused to herd the animals, he went into a tirade. She knew she took a chance that day when she went to worship under the tree, but how could she disobey Jesus? He had given His life for her.

The next day, the rest of the family went to the market while Kulwa and the stepfather remained at home. In the evening when they returned, no one could find Kulwa. Her stepfather said he had no idea where she had gone. As darkness approached, the animals came home without her. Sensing that something had gone terribly wrong, her mother started searching the surrounding area frantically, but to no avail. That night, her mother could not sleep wondering about her daughter. In the morning, she gathered some neighbors to help her. Soon they found Kulwa's body in a small stand of trees nearby. She had been positioned in a noose to make it appear that she had hanged herself. However, a doctor's examination showed that she had been beaten on the head, probably with an iron bar.

The villagers were horrified at this brutal murder. The stepfather received a prison sentence, and the family moved away. Amos, grief stricken, cried over the death of his new daughter in Christ. When Paulo brought me the story, I sat in my office and wept. I thought of this new babe in Christ martyred for her faith. *What good can come of this?* I wondered. *Lord, please don't let the story end like this. Please let this young girl's blood be seed for the gospel.* With sadness in my heart, I left it in God's hands for Him to do His wonders.

The following summer on furlough, we visited our son Keith at Weimar College in California, where he was studying to become a pastor. While there, I told Kulwa's story in the Meadow Vista Adventist Church. Touched by this young girl's death, the members organized themselves into a team to do evangelistic meetings in Tupendane. They also promised that they would build a church. Such enthusiasm thrilled me!

We sent two more Bible workers to help Amos prepare for the meetings. By the time the American team left home, the new church building was 80 percent complete. Our family went to Tupendane a few days early to prepare for the meetings and brought an assistant, Emanuel Henry, who was a graduate of our training school, as well as a good equipment technician. We packed our faithful Unimog truck, the vehicle that we used to carry equipment to evangelistic meetings.

While Emanuel set up the sound system, I began to prepare the benches for the meetings. That would involve digging eighty holes for the legs and then putting slabs of wood on top of them to serve as benches. With a machete and a sharpened iron bar with which to dig, I started pounding the sun-baked ground. The clay ground seemed as hard as rock. By the time I finished three holes, three large blisters spread out across my hand.

I'm an accountant. I admit it; I have soft hands. *I wonder what it will be like to have eighty blisters after eighty holes.* Suddenly, a voice behind me asked, "Do you need some help? I am the village chairman." I praised God for His mercy! Soon, a team of ten men began digging holes so fast that I could hardly keep up with them in nailing together the wood slabs that would serve as benches. We had been praying for a miracle. Surely I had experienced the first one. The village leader and all these men were Muslims, yet they gladly helped me set up for Christian evangelistic meetings. Amazing! What would God do next?

Tupendane is part of a three-village district called Mtandika. We arranged to hire a truck to bring people from the other two villages to our meetings each evening. The next afternoon when our team arrived from America, we wondered whether we would have much of a crowd. Their bus arrived late from Dar, and by the time they reached the meeting site, Emanuel had stalled as long as he could with nature videos. To our amazement, a crowd of nearly a thousand people waited! Keith preached a sermon about Daniel 2.

The team that came with Keith included David and Phyllis Smith and two children, Arnold and Stacy Hooker and their daughter, Emil and Elena Maghier, plus three young women. David and Keith alternated in preaching every other night. All three of the men worked on finishing the church. The women did the cooking as well as house-to-house visitation. We held separate meetings for the children, but used generators and projectors in both meetings to keep the attendance up. However, after only two days, we began to hear rumors circulating through the village. "Watch out for these white people! They want to get the village children separated so they can suck out their blood!" Amazingly, the Muslim leaders of the area made public announcements stating that these rumors were absurd.

Early on during the meetings, we gathered as a team around Kulwa's grave and prayed for God to work miracles in this dark village. Unfortunately, by the third night, we received a visit from the police. Although in Tanzania, night meetings in public areas are technically illegal, the requirements are often waived when we do nighttime projection or when we hold meetings in remote villages.

Because we did not have a waiver, the police insisted we must go to the regional headquarters in Iringa to request special permission. Obviously, someone who didn't like our meetings had complained to the police. We really needed the projection to hold our crowd, so we made it a matter of special prayer. When I visited the secretary of Mtandika, who was a Muslim, he insisted on accompanying me to visit the police. I wondered what he would say.

As we entered the police headquarters in Iringa the next day, the Mtandika secretary said, "You stay out here. I'll handle this." From outside the office, I heard him make an amazing plea, "Why are you police troubling these people? They present very nice meetings. I insist that they be allowed to continue after dark. Now, write the permission in a letter so I can take it with me!" Speechless, I heard this Muslim man defending our meetings. As we left with the permission letter in hand, I quietly thanked God. Surely, He has a thousand ways.

After an afternoon swim in the river near our hotel, we had a visit from the hotel management. "Don't swim in that river again," they warned. "Don't you know the river is infested with crocodiles?" As I visited with them, they told me a little about the local crocodiles. The year before, seven people died in crocodile attacks in the valley. However, this year there had not been a single one so far. They also warned us that the Muslim priests employed witchcraft to use the crocodiles to eliminate their enemies. Foolishly, I shrugged off the warning as just another story.

The next day, Amos's ten-year-old son went fishing in the river. Perhaps he could catch a fish to add to the family's food supply for the day. This same river had claimed the lives of Paulo's two sons a few years earlier. Suddenly, a huge crocodile lunged out of the water and grabbed Amos's son. As they entered the water again, the boy struggled helplessly. The crocodile's jaw enclosed the boy's entire

chest. His arm already reached far down the animal's throat. In panic, the boy thrashed desperately, making the teeth bite deeper. With no other human nearby, the boy had no hope for survival.

Maasai women who walked four hours to learn more about Jesus after hearing the meetings through the horn speakers.

Then suddenly the crocodile spit him out! Some speculated that his flailing arm caused water to get into the crocodile's lungs, which caused the beast to spit him out. I cannot say, but I believe the Lord intervened to spare the boy's life. No one could call this just good luck. More than answered prayer, God gave us a genuine miracle. Satan wanted to show that our God has no power to protect His people. But, instead, God proved that He could indeed perform wonders. The boy spent a few days in the hospital and will carry the scars for the rest of his life. However, he will always be a living testimony to the power of God's protecting angels.

Our meetings had reached the halfway point when we saw the next miracle. As we organized our various teams for building, cooking, and teaching that morning, a line of four Maasai women marched into our area. "In our village, we heard your meetings through your horn speakers in the night. We came as representatives. Please teach us more about Jesus," they explained to our team through Watson, our translator.

"Where are you from?" we asked. "We have walked since sunrise to reach here," they replied. Now it was about 10:00 A.M., so they walked for four hours to reach us. Watson and I looked at each other in wonder. Our horn speakers were good, but not that good. Knowing Maasai women walked fast, we concluded they'd walked at least twelve miles since daybreak. We knew they could not hear our speakers that far away. Another miracle from God! We got out our picture roll as Phyllis and Stacy told them more about Jesus, and Watson translated. They listened earnestly, asking questions from time to time. After lunch, they disappeared into the bush as mysteriously as they had come. They said they would be back the next day with more people.

As the truck pulled in at the meeting site that evening with its passengers from the two neighboring villages, I could see that our crowd had diminished from the previous evening. Arnold Hooker stayed at his usual post, welcoming people to the meeting. He took a special interest in a small crowd of young Maasai men who attended our meetings.

Seeing this tall American, the Maasai decided to test him to see who had the higher status in life. "How many wives do you have?" they asked. They waited in anticipation to see how many women he commanded in his life. "One," he responded. The leader of the band, a handsome and talented young warrior, spat on the ground and replied arrogantly, "I've got two so far." He frowned at Arnold as if to say, "You're not so important, big boy."

"How many cows do you have?" came the next logical question. "None. I don't own any cows," Arnold responded. They choked in disbelief at his answer. Now, they looked at him with something between disgust and sympathy as they tried to imagine this poor penniless American who didn't even have one cow. A herd of cows is a Maasai's bank account.

Leaving Arnold, they came over to talk to me. Now they had another agenda. Seeing the pitiful poverty of Americans, they decided to make us an offer we could not refuse. The leader approached me confidently, and after a brief welcome, he came to the point. Motioning toward the six young women in our group, he said, "I'll give you fifty cows, and you can choose which of those six girls I will take for a wife." I suppose he expected me to say he could have two or three for that price. Instead, thinking that he might be joking with me, I laughed and said, "That's not enough! You'll have to do better than that!"

Insulted, he looked at me with narrowed eyes. Standing to his full height, he said, "OK, I'll give you fifty cows and two thousand dollars for one of those girls." Now, as he stared intensely at me, I began to realize he meant business. He looked over the women again. I remembered traveling with Reuben across Tanzania and listening to his many stories about the Maasai.

My mind flashed back to a night on the Tanzania-Kenya border. We were staying in a guesthouse while waiting for our books to clear the border. After checking into the room, Reuben told me that he had left his backpack in the truck. Handing him the keys, I told him to go and get it. "Are you kidding?" he responded. "There's a Maasai guard out there with a spear. They never miss. He won't hesitate to spear me through in a second if I go out there. Those people fear nothing. They are ruthless." I looked at him in surprise, "Will he spear me?" I asked. "No, you're white; he'd be afraid of getting in trouble." So I went to the truck and got Reuben's pack, keeping a careful lookout for the guard.

Because I had no experience dealing with Maasai, these stories had given me a healthy fear of them. Now, I wondered what could stop him from taking whichever girl he wanted by force and running away with her. Fear took over—and that's when I totally blew it! I looked straight at him and said, "If you steal any of these girls, you will spend the rest of your life in prison." The young man looked down and wandered back to his group. Then, as if I not done enough damage already, I told the girls and their mothers to be careful and asked the village chairman to publicly ask people not to bother the girls. As I watched the mothers and daughters walking in a tight pack ready for an attack at any moment, I realized how I had terrified them. Besides that, I had just chased at least five of our attendees away from the meetings. I wondered how I could ever undo the damage I had caused. I left it with my God to sort out. (I learned later that the Maasai are usually honest in their dealing. This young man was simply suggesting a business deal.)

On Friday, we went to visit the Maasai village where the people had heard the meeting through our horn speakers. We had to drive a distance, walk some distance, and finally cross a river before we reached them. Steven, their spiritual leader, later attended our meetings. He told how he longed to have us come and teach the gospel in the eleven small Maasai villages on that side of the river. We knelt under a tree asking God to open the way for light to come to the Maasai of those villages.

The next morning, after our first worship service in the new church, we baptized twenty-eight new believers in the river. For us, this became a special day. Three young women from the evangelistic team also chose to be baptized, including our own daughter, April. Most of the village turned out to witness the baptism. They also saw the first four Maasai baptized that day. What a day of rejoicing! We remembered the precious miracles we had witnessed during the meetings. This became a sweet day for our team that had worked so hard and for Amos, who pioneered in this village. That evening the head man of Mtandika district confessed his own newfound faith in Jesus in front of all his constituents. We praised God.

Several months later, we returned and conducted a baptism of twenty more Maasai and eventually built a church for them. On the day of that baptism, God saved one more miracle just for me. As I looked over the crowd that day, I saw the young Maasai warrior whom I had insulted. I went to him and pleaded with him to forgive me for speaking to him the way I did. He acted embarrassed because he had never seen someone humble himself in this way. As I turned away, praying that somehow God could turn my mistake into good, the warrior spoke. "When will the next baptism be?" he asked. "I would like to be included on that day." I wanted to leap for joy! God is so good! In spite of our weaknesses and mistakes, He still uses us to do His will.

No longer do I weep for Kulwa. The world didn't take much notice of her passing, but to me, she's a hero. She probably never rode in a car. Never saw a movie. Didn't know anything about laptop computers. Perhaps she never even attended school. But in the eyes of heaven, I believe God marked her grave for a special day soon to come. She died a martyr's death for her faith, and her reward will be great. When she sees the harvest of Maasai in heaven, I know she will rejoice. How do we measure the eternal joy that results from faithfully serving Jesus now?

Chapter 13
WITCHES AND WITCHCRAFT

I am amazed that in recent years, witches and witchcraft have come to be regarded as popular and innocent to our society. Children's fiction has given the next generation the idea that witchcraft is just for fun and cannot really hurt anyone. However, here in Africa, we deal with it on a daily basis. I can assure you witchcraft has only one side—a very evil one.

Satan works through witchcraft, which the Bible states is an abomination to God. Let me share stories from people I know and trust, including former witches, clearly illustrating that witchcraft is a tool of Satan.

I confess that when I first came to Tanzania, I discounted virtually all of the witchcraft stories as fables. However, one day the president of one of the conferences took me aside. "Brother Mosier, you don't believe these stories of witchcraft, but I can tell you that these things constantly happen. You need to understand in order to save yourself much trouble in the future." He proceeded to share several stories from his own experience to convince me of the reality of witchcraft.

One Sabbath morning in church, this pastor preached about the sin of witchcraft. After the sermon, the members filed by him with greetings on the way out of church. After everyone had left the building, the head elder, who had purposely remained behind, grabbed the pastor and said, "Who told you about me?"

The pastor answered, "What are you talking about? Nobody has told me anything about you."

"Oh yes they did—or you would not have preached about witchcraft today. Someone has told you," the elder continued.

"Brother, why don't you tell me all that you mean. Then I'll understand what is upsetting you."

The church elder began to explain, "You see, I was a witch for many years. Then, I believed in God and became a Christian, finally joining the church. I got rid of all my witchcraft fetishes except for my traveling tools. I didn't think keeping them would hurt anything. I have a root in my pocket." He showed the pastor the shriveled up piece of root in his pocket. "When I want to travel to other places, like Kenya or even Europe, I just talk to the root. The root communicates to the gourd I keep at home. Then, the gourd talks back to the root, which turns into a hyena, and I climb on its back. We can go anywhere I want. After your sermon today, I can see that I cannot go to heaven if I keep using these things. I want to quit now!"

The pastor instructed the elder to go outside and confess his sin before all of the members and also to the Lord. Then, he asked the elder to get the gourd from his house. After praying, they lit a small fire and put the gourd on it. The gourd jumped around a bit on the fire, and some weird shrieks filled the air. Finally the gourd simply burned up. The root, however, did not cooperate as well. When they put it on the fire, that shriveled up old root seemed to have a big sprinkler system inside. Water poured out of it and extinguished the fire immediately. The pastor then called for kerosene. They lighted another fire, poured kerosene on the flames, and threw the root in once more. Again, devilish shrieks and screams filled the air as the root slowly burned up. After that, the elder became free from the control of witchcraft. This pastor had seen these things with his own eyes. He explained to me how fearful that elder felt about losing his salvation. He told me that the elder truly believed he traveled to all those places in the night. He had actually transacted business in these faraway places. Satan's deceptions had sincerely deceived this church elder.

The next two stories were told by Pastor Mtenzi, an experienced Tanzanian pastor with whom I have worked for many years.

The first one involved a very dedicated church planter with whom he worked closely. The man had moved to an unentered area to start a new congregation. As he sat in his home one evening soon after his arrival in the village, strange things started to happen around his house. A basket on the table started spinning in circles all by itself. Another basket began to move across the floor and return to its place all by itself.

The man did not hesitate. He offered a quick prayer, picked up his Bible, and began preaching. "I am so glad you have come to my house today. I want to tell you about Jesus," he said, although he could not see to whom he was preaching. He shared what the Bible says about sin and how Jesus can forgive us and give us new lives in Him. As he preached, the baskets stopped moving. "Now, I see that you are listening," said the man to his unseen guests. He continued his sermon. After an hour, he went to bed and eventually forgot about the incident.

After a few months, the church planter held evangelistic meetings, and several people chose to be baptized. After the baptism, one of the new members came to his home to visit and thank him. "It's good to be back in your home again," he said to the church planter.

"But this is the first time you have ever been in my home," he responded.

"No, it is not," said the new member. "Don't you remember the night when you were here all alone and the baskets started moving around in your house? Two of us witches had come to frighten you and scare you away from our village. We did not want you to tell people here about Jesus. When you started to preach, my friend became bored and flew out the window, but I stayed and listened to your entire sermon. Since then, I wanted so much to know Jesus and have my sins forgiven. I attended your meetings and gave my heart to Jesus. Since my baptism, I have peace. I have left that evil life and find joy in Jesus."

"Oh, yes, I had forgotten all about that night. What you say must be true," said the church planter. "I have told no one else about that experience, and you could not know it any other way unless you had spent time with me that night. Praise God that you have been saved by the blood of Jesus!" They rejoiced together.

On another occasion, Pastor Mtenzi preached an evangelistic series in an area of Tanzania known as having the strongest witchcraft in the country. During the sermon about witchcraft, a practicing witch happened to be walking by. The words that Pastor Mtenzi spoke riveted his attention. "Jesus has power. He is stronger than any witchcraft or sin in your life. If you accept Him, He can help you escape your life of witchcraft and forgive your sins."

As the witch heard these words, hope sprang up in his heart. He hated his life of service to the devil, but he did not know how to stop. He feared that if he left Satan's service, he would be killed. He asked one of the church members standing nearby, "Is this true and possible what this pastor teaches? Can I really get away from my witchcraft?"

"Yes, it is true. Wait until the sermon is over, and you can visit with the pastor yourself," the church member replied.

As soon as the meeting was finished, the witch talked with Pastor Mtenzi, who explained how Jesus is the way out of witchcraft and sin. The witch believed and was jubilant because he now had hope! He could leave his evil life of witchcraft and curses behind! "I accept Jesus now. I believe He can save me. Please, Pastor, come to my house and destroy all the witchcraft tools that I have been using," he pleaded.

The next morning, Pastor Mtenzi met with the witch. The choir and some of the church leaders accompanied Pastor Mtenzi and walked with him to the witch's home. They prayed together before they started. Word had spread like a wildfire through the village about what was to take place; already, spectators had gathered.

As the Christian group neared the house, people began to warn the team not to go near the witch's property. "He has a big snake that guards his property. Anyone who goes near will be chased away by the snake," explained a villager. Another said, "I once took a basket from his house, but when I went home, the basket stuck to my head. I could not remove it. I finally took a goat to that witch and begged him for forgiveness. Then the basket came off my head. Be careful!"

When the house came into view, Pastor Mtenzi paused to see which members were willing to go into the house with him. "This is a job for the pastor!" they declared in unison. At least one said, "I have not made everything right in my life. Even my tithe is not up-to-date. I cannot go in there." So Pastor Mtenzi went on alone with the witch. The witch began trembling as they got close to the house. "Be careful! That snake could be anywhere here. Now that I have become a Christian, I also fear it may turn against me."

Warily, they came up to the door of the house, and the former witch began looking around nervously. As he tiptoed through the door with Pastor Mtenzi, he shouted, "There he is—coiled in the corner! Don't go near him!"

Pastor Mtenzi's eyes were getting used to the darkness, but he could see only a large coil of rope on the floor. He started walking over to pick up the rope, saying, "It's just a coil of rope, not a snake."

"Don't you see him? Are you crazy? He is going to bite you!" shouted the witch.

Pastor Mtenzi simply picked up the rope and took it outside to burn with the rest of the fetishes. Then their trouble began. First they faced much trouble burning the fetishes. They finally had to make a big fire to keep the rope from putting out the fire. Suddenly, he heard a small explosion in the middle of the fire. Immediately, the witch collapsed on the ground and to all appearances lay dead. Promptly Pastor Mtenzi began to pray. Soon the man revived. Finally, they managed to burn the rope. By God's grace that witch never again faced trouble from the evil spirits.

From these stories, it should be obvious that no one should ever play with witchcraft. The evil angels will try to convince you that you are unable to escape from their clutches. And, without the power of Jesus, a person can be hopelessly trapped! Christians are never safe to leave unconfessed sins remaining in our lives.

Satan also uses illusions to frighten people and keep them under his control. However, to say that all of these phenomena are illusions would not be true. One of our evangelism instructors, Watson Kiwovele, worked as a church planter for years and faced mysterious events in his own home. He felt fingers clutching his throat and strangling him. He could not see who was strangling him, but the icy hands had a mighty grip on his throat. The same thing happened to another of our evangelism teachers during our meetings in the village of Kisada.

I have not included the bloody, gruesome stories connected with witchcraft of which there are plenty. People regularly pay for curses to be put on other people, sometimes even causing their deaths. Then the victims must find a more powerful witch to curse their enemy in return. This becomes an endless cycle of hatred and revenge. No wonder Satan uses these methods. Certainly, exaggerations abound and fantastic stories circulate, but the fact is that Satan uses witchcraft to exert his power over the people. The villagers fear

Ephraim, the witch doctor, holding the fetish that we burned.

witchcraft for good reasons. Satan has power. However, God's power is much stronger. When we rest in Jesus day by day, we do not need to fear it.

Ephraim, a powerful witch, lived in the village of Matema, Tanzania. People feared him and would sometimes bow to him as he passed by. He made his living cursing people, but also used certain herbs and plants for healing people.

One of Ephraim's powerful fetishes was a two-foot stick wrapped in python skin. Satan often manifested his power through this stick. If the stick rattled on the table during the night, it meant another witch was flying over his area. He could point the stick toward the sky and force the lesser witch to come down to his home. Then, Ephraim would fine the less-powerful witch for passing without permission, scold him, and let him go. This helped him retain his status as the most powerful witch in the area.

If someone in the village had been cursed, they could call Ephraim to help them locate the offender. They could call together a group of possible offenders. Ephraim would pass his stick in front of them. The stick would pull the guilty party out of the line so he could be punished. Another fetish Ephraim used was a little animal skin with beads glued to it. For him, this worked as a computer. As he passed it before people, it would tell him which ones were witches and the amount of power they had. Ephraim had it all. Power, fame, fortune, and respect. However, all this power did not satisfy his soul; he wished for joy and peace in his life.

One day our missionary, Richard Jackson, stopped at Ephraim's door to see whether he would like to take Bible studies. When he saw Richard's happy, smiling face, and the Bible in his hand, Ephraim felt an overwhelming desire for something better.

Soon, every week the two of them began studying together. Ephraim was irresistibly drawn to the truths of the Bible. Some time later, when Sylvester Temboh and I held evangelistic meetings there, Ephraim experienced conversion. God gave him a new heart. After we arrived, he met with us to see when we could come to his home and burn his fetishes.

Finally, the day came, and Richard led us along the winding path to Ephraim's home. We met his wife, Marieta. He showed us the fetishes and explained what he had used them for. Then he started hacking the stick to pieces with a machete. He never hesitated. He felt very happy when we lit it on fire. As we watched the fire do its cleansing work, a man came seeking his services. Ephraim explained that he was now a Christian and didn't do that kind of work anymore. The man pled with him to do just one more job. "Where will we go for help when you are gone?" he wailed. I could see that

Ephraim had a loyal clientele as the man simply would not leave him alone.

At the conclusion of our meetings, Ephraim was baptized, along with fifteen others. Sadly, after he was no longer the most powerful person in the village, his wife left him. Ephraim came to our evangelism training school to learn to win others to Christ. After returning to Matema, he started visiting another village nearby to share his faith. Today, Ephraim is a Bible worker in Rukwa Valley, where he shares his love of Jesus door to door.

Ephraim gave up the power, respect, money, and fame to become a humble disciple of Christ. He told us a few terrible stories of what he did as a witch, but he doesn't like to talk about it much. As another converted witch once said, "Jesus is more better." Now, as he goes about his work of winning others to Christ, Ephraim's soul is satisfied.

Chapter 14
NEEDS BEYOND TANZANIA

"Barry, it's time for you to expand your ministry. Tanzania's neighboring countries need help too."

I sat in the office of Geoffrey Mbwana, the president of the newly formed East-Central African Division. We had formed a close friendship while he served as the leader of the Tanzania Union Mission. Pastor Mbwana possessed a contagious passion for evangelism.

I was in Nairobi, Kenya, again, and what a difference time and experience had made in me. The panic I had felt on my first trip when I had been delayed in returning to Jared in a strange and dangerous city had been replaced by trust. My travels around Africa taught me to work hand-in-hand with my Savior, learning to depend wholly on Him.

Pastor Mbwana had e-mailed me a few months earlier, asking that I come to Nairobi to discuss the needs of this brand-new Division. Kibidula's ministry had crept across the borders of Tanzania before, but nothing like we were talking about now! Pastor Mbwana and his team had five specific requests for help in as many countries as possible:

bicycles for gospel workers
Bible picture rolls
books for the publishing program
Bible study lessons in the local languages, and
church roofs

Their goal was simple, and it was the same as ours: tools in the hands of laypeople to help them spread the gospel. These needs seemed overwhelming, but I knew God could provide if it was His will.

Over the next two years, the Lord opened the way for us to provide thousands of picture rolls for teaching the Bible to children and adults. Kibidula's publishing ministry expanded rapidly in Tanzania, but we also shipped books to Kenya, Uganda, and Democratic Republic of Congo (DRC). After introducing Pastor Mbwana to Light Bearers Ministry, he arranged with them to ship Bible studies to countries across the Division. Roofs Over Africa provided Kibidula with iron sheets to roof fourteen hundred churches throughout Tanzania, Uganda, and Malawi. Finally, we submitted a request to ASI for one hundred thousand dollars' worth of bicycles for frontline gospel workers in war-torn countries of the East-Central Africa Division. We prayed, and God answered. The entire amount was approved, and my heavenly Father met our needs again! During the next year and a half, 1,150 bicycles were distributed across the Division.

In October 2003, the East-Central Africa Division asked Keith and me to report about the evangelism training and church planting work of Kibidula to the Union officers at their year-end meeting. At the very moment Keith put up the first slide of the presentation about church planters, the computer went dead. Keith, a bit shaken as he now faced all these leaders without his slides, moved ahead without them. He explained how Kibidula placed trained laypeople in unentered areas, raised up new congregations, and then worked with them to construct new churches and train local leaders.

When we took the computer to a store for repair, we found out that the hard drive had died on the spot. Only one year old, the laptop had given me no problems. Why did it die at the very moment that we put up the first slide on church planting?

"I believe that Satan hates this church planting work intensely," Keith observed. "Dad, you use that computer most of the day each day for work. I'm sure Satan killed that hard drive right at that crucial moment."

"I don't see any other way to explain it, Son. Satan did not want these Union and Division leaders to be inspired to train laymen to plant churches. Then, laymen across this whole Division would catch fire for spreading the gospel. He hates to give up his dark strongholds to the gospel message. Obviously, he fears this church planting work," I answered.

As we relaxed in the evenings, we were somewhat overwhelmed by all the invitations to start projects in the various unions. Finally, Pastor Masasia Makulambizia, the president of the North East Congo Attached Territory (NECAT), came to our room to talk. He told us about the challenges in his area. The war had crippled the work in the eastern side of Congo. To the west and north, great numbers of people in the lowland jungles had never heard the gospel. As he pleaded with Keith and me to come and help with the work in Congo, he touched something deep inside of Keith. Keith felt God's Spirit telling him that God had chosen this to be his place of work. He saw clearly that after studying for the ministry, he must return to NECAT to work as a missionary for God.

Three years later, Sylvester Temboh and I attended a unionwide meeting in Tanzania for Global Pioneers. Global Pioneers is an organization of church planters coordinated by the Seventh-day Adventist Church. The Pioneers function much like the lay missionaries sent out by Kibidula. We brought one hundred applications for our evangelism school, but were not prepared for the response. As Sylvester and I left each meeting, people mobbed us for application forms. Our presentations during the meetings only enhanced their desire for evangelism education. "You mean that even if we have only standard seven education [seventh grade], we may come to your school?" they asked in amazement. "Most of us are farmers without high-school degrees. We lost hope to obtain further education." We made another two hundred copies of the application form and quickly gave those away also.

In our room that night, Sylvester said, "If the desire for evangelism training is this strong in Tanzania where we already have an evangelism school, what is it like in other countries? These laymen long for the chance to learn better soul-winning skills."

Pastor Musema from the Division office agreed. "We need this kind of training all around our Division. We have global pioneer programs and budgets, but no provision for training. Please, could you provide this training in other parts of the Division? In fact, I would be grateful if you would submit a curriculum for training. I would then present it to the Division as the official training program for Global Pioneers."

Pastor Musema, a former president of North East Congo, explained how much the evangelism training was needed in that particular area. "In fact, why don't we travel there together next February to gather bicycle reports and see the needs firsthand?"

"That sounds great to me," I replied as I began to glimpse the magnitude of the need.

Arriving home again, I did some research about DRC and was amazed at how little I knew. The Congo River Basin in the north and west especially intrigued me. One million square miles of rain-forest jungle drains into that river. Few roads exist and river transportation dominates the Congo River Basin. The rest of the country relies heavily on airplanes to transport people and goods.

In November 2006, DRC had their first peaceful elections in more than forty years. Sylvester and I breathed a sigh of relief concerning our upcoming trip to visit the country. Five million people had died in the war during the preceding ten years—most from disease and starvation. Considering that is the largest death count of any war since World War II, we were anxious about the trip. As I read some of the gruesome accounts of rape, murder, and conscription of child soldiers, I could understand why DRC had the worst human rights record in the world during that time. We were thankful for the returning peace.

In February, we traveled through Rwanda by bus with Pastor Musema. Sylvester and I were in awe of the beauty of the country. The farm fields covered the mountainous slopes like a patchwork quilt.

As we crossed the border into Goma, DRC, we were not prepared for the grim contrast. Burned vehicles still lay partly buried in their lava tombs as a constant reminder of the volcanic eruption in 2002. Soldiers with automatic weapons were prevalent. United Nations troops passed by in vehicles with large guns mounted in the back. Refugee camps dominated the outskirts of Goma, containing tens of thousands of villagers who fled before the rebels. We could see that keeping peace in DRC was not an easy task for the seventeen thousand United Nations peacekeeping forces in the country.

The next day a hero's welcome awaited us at the Conference office. Members lined the road waiving flowers and singing praises to God. Six church planters presented their reports about the bicycles they had received. "Thank you for my bicycle. I am now reaching farther than I could before. Fifteen people have now joined the church as a result of this bicycle," reported one pioneer. The reports each mentioned from five to fifteen new church members. I thanked God for enabling us to put bicycles into the hands of these dedicated laypeople.

In the afternoon, I explained to the Union leaders the ideas that Keith wanted to implement in NECAT. "If God opens the way,

Keith will train laypeople in evangelism and then employ them as church planters to reach unentered areas and assist in building new churches. He hopes to rebuild the publishing ministry with free Bible study tracts in the local language and books for colporteurs to sell. Finally, he believes that medical missionary work and agriculture would help to open the work along the Congo River in the Upper Congo Field."

Pastor Makulambizia replied, "Those are exactly the areas we need help with. Please, please come! Just come. We need help."

The next day at the airport, where we were to take another flight, military helicopters and airplanes were everywhere. Soldiers hid behind piles of sandbags as they guarded the airport. As we waited for the plane to arrive, I chatted with a lady next to me who had an injured leg. "What happened to your leg?" I queried.

"I was in an airplane accident a couple of years ago," was her response. "The plane we were in didn't make it to the Goma airport, but landed in the forest near here. I survived the accident, but my leg was badly injured." I swallowed as I thought about my upcoming flight.

A few hours later, we landed in the capital city of Kinshasa. The city of more than eight million people sprawls along the Congo River in western Africa. There the bicycle reports encouraged us once again. However, my Swahili was of little help to me in this French- and Lingala-speaking section of the country.

A few days later, we finally reached Kisangani. As people stared at me through the vehicle window, I wondered how they felt when they saw a white person. Early Europeans had ruthlessly plundered DRC. Through forced slavery, they killed an estimated ten million people—about half the population of the country. I longed to offset this evil of the past with a message of love and hope.

We met global pioneers who traveled two hundred to three hundred miles one way to bring their bicycle reports. I found that I could communicate again! My Swahili did not match theirs exactly, but I could get by. Then we traveled into the country to visit churches. Most of them were pitiful mud huts; iron-sheet roofs were almost unknown. Wherever we went, the members pleaded for us to come back to help.

I learned a lot on that journey. I could not erase from my memory the stark needs of DRC. As I explained the hardships of the people to Marybeth back at Kibidula, we started praying about whether God wanted us in DRC. Perhaps Keith needed us to help start the work there. We knew that God would make clear His will for us.

Chapter 15
FEAR

A highlight of our Kibidula schedule arrived again—the semi-annual meeting of our lay missionaries. They trekked from their remote stations to report how the work in each territory had progressed. At these meetings, we conducted seminars to encourage and assist the lay missionaries and also paid their wages for the following six months.

So, on a Friday, Sylvester Temboh and I each made two trips to Mafinga to collect the twenty-six lay missionaries who had traveled there by bus. As we pulled up to our office, there were shouts of joy and many hugs as we greeted each other. *"Habari za siku nyingi?* [What is the news of many days?]" The automatic reply was, "*Nzuri* [Good]."

Although tired from their journey, the lay missionaries stayed up much of the night sharing stories about the progress of God's work in their areas. The next morning during Sabbath School, they gave their testimonies and stories of the previous six months. Happy to see our missionaries again, I checked each one off in my mind as I surveyed the group. I made a mental note that Yohana and Mejoni from the Chunya area were missing. This often happens due to un-reliable transportation.

A few lay missionaries and other guests were invited to join us for Sabbath lunch. Finally, Marybeth announced, "Come and eat." I rejoiced in eager expectation of a good Sabbath meal.

Then my cell phone rang. "Hello, Yohana speaking. I was de-layed along the way, but I am now at end of the road. Come and pick me up." Normally, I would have been happy to hear that my

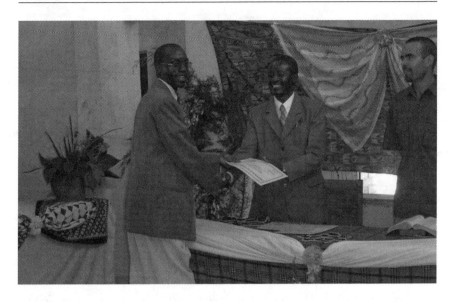

Sylvester Temboh and Jason Fournier presenting a diploma to an evangelism school graduate.

"lost sheep" had finally arrived at the meeting, but not right at that moment. Our guests already waited around the table for prayer. A trip to "the end of the road" meant a cold lunch and a late arrival for my next meeting. Stephano Kasiri, my faithful book shipper in Dar, introduced me to his new bride, and I looked forward to hearing all about the wedding! The steaming food on the table beckoned me. *Surely, Yohana won't mind if I take just one quick plateful before leaving,* I rationalized. So, I quickly loaded my plate and sat down.

The fork was just reaching my mouth when the phone rang again. I hardly recognized Yohana's voice as he shouted into his phone in terror.

"Hurry! I am running for my life! Thieves are chasing me! They will kill me! Please hurry!"

I dropped my fork on my plate and leaped up, giving a hasty explanation to Marybeth. Stephano grabbed a machete as he hopped into the car beside me. We prayed a quick prayer before the engine roared to life and we raced out the driveway.

The rainy season had just started, so we blasted through several large puddles along the way. The eight miles to the end of the road seemed so far away. I leaned slightly forward as I gripped the steering wheel tightly and stepped on the accelerator. The grassland area behind us, we started to enter the large pine forest that covers much of the Mafinga countryside.

Can this really be happening on our Kibidula road? We had not heard of such a thing in recent times. People frequently walked in from the end of the forest road. *Is it possible that armed bandits are attacking Yohana?* Just the thought of it made me hurry faster.

As I rounded a corner, I saw Yohana, still running. I wondered how he had gotten this far on foot. I jumped out of the car, and Yohana literally collapsed into my arms. Covered with sweat, he was completely exhausted. He panted as he tried desperately to explain, "If you didn't get here . . . by the time I got to that corner . . . I was going to give up . . . and let him kill me. . . . So happy . . . to see you."

As I held Yohana up, I glanced up and saw his lone pursuer still running toward us from some distance down the road. Amazed at the persistence of his attacker and that he did not fear to approach our vehicle, I helped Yohana onto the car seat. Then I turned again to face the assailant. *But wait. He looks familiar to me.*

Is it possible? Yes, I could make out the features of his face. I recognized Mejoni, the other lay missionary from the Chunya area. As he approached, I looked back at Yohana and saw the look of recognition and incredulity cross his face. Although they worked many miles apart, the two were good friends. Then we laughed and laughed together. A moment before, Yohana thought his life would come to

an end, and now he could not stop laughing.

As we drove home, Yohana explained what had happened. They had traveled separately and were unaware of each others' proximity. As Yohana dropped from the *dala dala* (mini bus) at the end of the road, he saw a hunter carrying a machete, accompanied by a dog. At that point fear entered his mind, and he started his journey into the forest afraid. After he hurried down the road, he heard a shout behind him. Looking back, he saw someone waving his arm and shouting at him. Fear gripped him in its embrace. His poor eyesight caused him to imagine the hunter coming his way with a machete and a dog. He turned in terror, running into the deep forest. Then he called me to come and save him.

At each turn in the road, he ran faster, hoping

Yohana, the lay missionary who fled from his companion.

to shake his relentless pursuer. However, the "killer" continued to bear down on him, waving and shouting. With each shout, Yohana lost his ability to reason until he fell into a complete state of panic.

Thus fear can control us and make us unable to reason. Fear caused him to run away from help, when help followed him. So, Yohana forgot all about faith in God and ran away from his own friend—just because of fear. I've told the story many times to various congregations to encourage our members to be people of faith, not of fear—and each time we had a chuckle at Yohana's expense.

Several years later, while driving from Nairobi to Dar, I learned my own lesson about fear. Pastor Mtenzi and I had just attended Division meetings and now were traveling back to Tanzania. We had important business the next day and knew we must reach Dar that night. However, we faced many delays along the way. Soon darkness came and we still had far to go. Pulling a trailer behind the Land Cruiser slowed us even more. As we drove through some barren, hilly country, I saw headlights approaching in my rearview mirror. I slowed a bit to let the vehicle pass, and as they did, I noticed that the car had four men in it and was licensed in Kenya. After passing me, they mysteriously slowed down and I wondered why. After following them for a little way, I passed them to get back to my normal speed.

However, I had not gone far before they passed me again and immediately slowed down again. This seemed like strange behavior, and I started to worry. We were traveling in a very remote area that would be a perfect location for a robbery.

I knew people in Kenya were frequently stopped and killed for their cars. In fact, Kenyans make Tanzanians nervous because they often act more aggressively than Tanzanians. Would these men try to rob me when we reached a certain place on the road? Now, adrenaline had my mind racing.

As we got to a straighter spot in the road, I told Pastor Mtenzi, "Hang on. We will pass these guys and leave them in the dust. They must be thieves." At that point, I slammed the pedal to the floor and raced past them. I continued at as high a speed as I dared until I could no longer see their lights behind me. Soon we reached a high single-lane bridge where an accident had cars backed up and waiting. As they cleared the accident, I saw the Kenyan vehicle pull up behind me.

Feeling quite safe with all these people around and the road blocked, I decided to go back and talk to them. "*Pole na safari* [Sorry for the journey]," I said as I came up to their window. "It looks like we have to wait a bit here."

"We don't mind relaxing for a bit," they said. "We have been scared to death driving through these hills alone since we are foreigners. We had hoped to drive together with you, but we couldn't catch you. You were really flying."

I felt foolish as I walked back to the car to tell Pastor Mtenzi what they said. After I explained it to him, he chuckled at bit. Then he looked at me and said, "Yes, Yohana."

I laughed at myself because I deserved the gentle rebuke for my lack of faith. I acted on the same fear I had laughed at Yohana for having.

Probably we all have. Let us pray that God will help us overcome our fears. "There is no fear in love; but perfect love casteth out fear" (1 John 4:18).

Chapter 16
WE'RE ALIVE!

When we trust in Jesus, He gives us courage in all emergencies. God will take charge of our minds and help us to make good, quick decisions. That's what happened to our precious daughter, April, on the day when our plane crashed at takeoff in Goma.

Moments after the airplane crashed, she left her seat and raced toward the front of the flaming DC-9. She cannot remember crossing the drop-off we encountered a few moments later. We will never know until heaven how her angel transported her over that section. She prayed as she went, *Lord, help us to get out of this plane.* However, as she reached the front of the economy-class section, she couldn't see any way out. *Am I trapped in this horrible fire? Am I going to die in here?* she asked herself.

Glancing down and to her right, she saw a crack on the right side of the plane—away from the worst of the fire. Taking in the situation in a glance, she realized that this might be her only way out.

"We must open this hole in the plane or we'll die!" she shouted in Swahili to a man who noticed the crack at the same time. They both started ripping at the crack with their bare hands, racing the flames as they tried to claw open a way of escape before the plane exploded. Surely angels must have helped them as handful by handful they pulled off hunks of the fuselage until the hole became big enough for April to get through. Diving headfirst through the hole, she became stuck at the waist.

But then someone inside pushed her. She could make it out. Slithering out onto a small pile of rocks, she never dreamed that this hole would be the way of escape for so many of the passengers, including her own parents. Leaping to her feet, she ran to a nearby flight attendant.

"My parents are still in the plane," she quickly explained.

"Run far away before the plane explodes!" ordered the flight attendant.

As April fled from the burning wreckage into the melee of people, she saw sights that she didn't want to remember. People trapped under the plane. Others horribly burned. Shocked, she saw Congolese soldiers passing her as they fled from the scene. *Shouldn't they be running the other way to help people?* she wondered.

April desperately scanned the crowd for any white face she could see. Then she spotted a Frenchman who had been sitting behind us in the plane. He had kicked out a window and forced his way out of the tiny hole, cutting his face in the process. Now, he waited anxiously for his friend to emerge from the burning plane. Finding a common language in Swahili, they both waited for a few seconds, staring hopefully at the opening in the plane. No friend and no parents came out, so they ran farther and farther from the wreckage. Their hopes faded as the plane seemed to be totally engulfed in flames. Surely no one could come out of there alive anymore. In despair, April wondered if she should just go back into the plane and join her parents.

Curious people scurried past them to get closer to the accident and see what had happened as smoke rose into the air like a signal to the whole city of the disaster that had just occurred. Grief stricken and in shock, April and the Frenchman wandered farther away from the scene. Soon a police vehicle spotted them and ordered them to get in the car.

"Please take me to ADRA [Adventist Development and Relief Agency]," April requested, "because my parents are dead." Still in shock from the accident, it hurt to even say these words; but who could possibly come out of that plane now? As the car raced her to the hospital, she wondered what she should do. Who would help her in this strange city? In this teeming mass of people and in a completely foreign country, she felt alone. Then her mind and trust turned to Jesus.

Marybeth and I looked back in disbelief as we saw the explosion that should have ended our lives. Our lack of glasses saved us from seeing much of the horror of the accident, but even a little sufficed. People, trapped under the plane, desperately tried to escape. At least one young man fled the crash with his shirt on fire. People cried out their grief as they sought loved ones who were now underneath the plane, some from the flaming market. The leaking fuel had done its work, and now the fire followed it everywhere. Ten thousand people raced toward the crash site, some to help, some to steal, but most to see the tragedy with their own eyes.

As we looked at the chaos, we wondered how we would ever find our children. Was April alive? Hysterically, we started asking people if they had seen our children, but no one seemed to pay much attention to us. Suddenly, the man who had taken Andrew walked up to us still carrying him in his arms.

"My baby! My baby!" Marybeth shouted as she reached frantically to take Andrew. The man turned away from her, unable to believe that this was really her child. He had been looking for an African mother to claim this little survivor. Clearly, he did not want to give Andrew to us. Then, as I felt my jacket pocket, I said, "Praise be to God!"

Through all the chaos, God had kept our passports safe in my pocket. When I showed Andrew's passport to the man, he happily handed him to Marybeth. Then, he grabbed my hand in a vice grip and started leading us away from the flaming wreckage of what had been Flight 122. Occasionally, he would say, "Be calm. Be calm."

But we didn't want to be calm! We looked everywhere for April.

As we stumbled past people, we asked in Swahili, "Have you seen a white girl wearing a red shirt?" But no one had. As we distanced ourselves from the crash, we passed a hysterical woman who was looking for her two children. I vaguely remembered two children besides Andrew in the plane, and I could only hope that someone had helped them out. Someone suggested that Andrew might be one of them, but the woman could see that he was not hers.

Soon an emergency vehicle raced up to us, and the police demanded that we get in.

"But we are still looking for our daughter," we insisted. Our pleas fell on deaf ears. Clearly irritated, the police insisted that we go with them, so we got into the vehicle, hoping that they might take us to April. Soon, we drove through the gate of HEAL Africa Hospital and went through a large complex of buildings to the emergency treatment area. As we sat to wait our turn, we continued our questions to others being treated after the crash.

"Did you see a white girl wearing a red shirt?" we inquired. Several people shook their heads. Most had injuries that were generally minor—because the seriously injured were already in the treatment rooms. Unknown to us, the hospital doctors were on strike. However, other employees on duty rose to the occasion as emergency vehicles continued to bring a steady stream of injured people to the hospital.

"Bring that one in first," came the order from somewhere inside one of the treatment rooms. I cringed as I saw a badly burned arm hanging from the moaning body on the stretcher. On the floor lay a body covered with a sheet, someone who no longer needed treatment.

A team of visiting doctors who had just arrived from Denver to do some teaching rushed into service. Seeing me sitting there, an

American man offered, "Here is my cell phone. Call anywhere in the world."

I stared at the cell phone in the outstretched hand in front of me for a moment, trying to gather my thoughts. My own cell phone and address book with the list of all my contacts remained in the burning plane.

Think, Barry, think, I told myself, but to no avail. "Thank you so much, but I don't know what to do with it. I can't remember even one number to call," I admitted.

One overpowering question still filled my mind. *Where is April?* Marybeth continued to ask the others around us for any information, and now her search was rewarded.

"Yes, I pushed your daughter out of the hole in the side of the plane," answered a Filipino man in English.

"Then she's alive!" Marybeth shouted as tears of joy coursed down her cheeks. We thanked him over and over. She was alive! Somewhere in this huge city, our April waited alone. But God kept her alive!

"Yes, she is OK," the man repeated. "We were trapped in the front of the plane. We could find no place for us to go, but we saw a crack and started opening it with our hands. She dived through the hole, and when she got stuck, I pushed her out. Then, with the help of others on the outside, we made the hole bigger."

As he continued his explanation, I glanced up, and even without my glasses I saw in the distance a short white girl in a red shirt being escorted toward us through the crowd. "April!" I shouted. Arms outstretched, I dodged hospital personnel, my feet seeming not even to touch the ground as I ran toward her.

"Daddy!" burst from her lips as she saw me coming. Here before her very eyes, she saw her father alive. Was it possible? April had remained brave up to now, but suddenly Daddy was in front of her.

Now, she could release the pent-up emotion that she had coura-geously suppressed since the crash. A wave of relief swept over her and tears poured down her cheeks as we embraced. "Oh, Daddy, I didn't know if you were still alive."

Then another shriek of joy. "Mommy! Mommy!" as she saw Mary-beth following me with Andrew in her arms. For her the horrible nightmare was over. As we locked in an embrace of love and relief, I noticed her companion. He was the Frenchman from the rear of the plane. His bloodstained face wore a beaming smile as he saw the reunion of parents and the young girl he had taken under his care. His kind duty was now over, and he could continue the search for his missing friend. We thanked him over and over as best we could through the universal language of heartfelt joy.

"We're all alive! A whole family coming out of an airplane crash! It's a miracle! We're all alive!" Marybeth repeated over and over as we sat back down, continuing to cling to each other. Could heaven be this sweet?

After April thanked the man again who helped push her out of the plane, we gathered for prayer. There in the midst of the patients waiting for treatment, we poured out our souls in heartfelt gratitude to God in prayer for sparing our lives. We knew why the plane had not exploded right away. God had intervened! There could be no other answer. We wanted to sing praises to His name as we started to recount to each other our experience since the crash. However, the overwhelming thought for each of us as we stared at and kept hugging each other was, "We're all alive! God is *sooooo* good!"

We concluded, incorrectly it turned out, that we were all unin-jured after the crash. Seeing all the wounded people around us, we decided that we should leave for the Union office and try to get word to Keith, who was probably already at the airport in Kisangani looking for us.

After leaving our names with hospital personnel, we hailed a taxi. Outside the hospital compound, the streets were filled with people. The taxi driver, taking in our situation, decided this was an emergency trip. He laid on the horn and the gas pedal as he raced through intersections at breakneck speed. Continually asking him to slow down, we hung on for dear life as we wondered whether we had survived an airplane crash only to die in a car wreck.

Finally, we arrived at the Union office and started limping painfully over the driveway of crushed volcanic rock. I still had only one shoe, and Marybeth was barefoot. Union employees poured out the doors with arms outstretched to greet us. They had heard that the plane had crashed and, seeing the smoke rising in the distance, were sure we were dead. Pastor Manyama was already on his way back to the airport to find out what had happened to us. His secretary, Solanje, who had helped with travel and other arrangements on all of my trips, wept for joy upon seeing us. They knew they were seeing a walking miracle.

After getting Keith's number, we tried to call him on a borrowed cell phone, but he did not answer. How could we get word to him? What had happened at the airport in Kisangani?

Chapter 17

ALL THINGS WORK TOGETHER FOR GOOD

"OK, Dad. I'll be there, and I can't wait to see you. I love you. Bye." Keith didn't know how close these came to being the last words that he ever spoke to me. He had been waiting for this day with anticipation. Now his family was coming to visit the project dear to his heart. He hoped and prayed for a positive experience in our visit so we'd join the project. With a light heart, he mounted his motorcycle to head for the airport.

After entering the airport, Keith sensed something was wrong. When he asked whether the flight had arrived, they referred him to the Hewa Bora desk. Although Hewa Bora means "best air," they gave him the worst news. "That plane crashed onto some buildings after takeoff and burst into flames. It's still burning now."

This news hit him like a hammer blow. "Are there any survivors?" he asked as his mind raced.

"A few people called saying they are OK, but we don't yet know any more than that," answered the attendant, her gaze at the floor.

"Were any of them *Wazungu* [white people]?" he inquired with panic rising in his voice.

"We don't know," was the quiet reply. "Were you waiting for someone on the plane?"

"I expected the four people that I am closest to in the whole world, my mom and dad and little brother and sister." Staggering away from the desk, Keith bought phone cards to make some calls. He held to a strong hope that we might have made it out, but had no way of knowing. Calling my cell phone, it seemed like an eternity as he waited for me to answer it. He felt like shouting, "Answer your phone, Dad! Be alive!" But the phone just kept ringing. With every ring, a little more of his hope drained away.

Questions tore at his mind. *Why? How could they die when they still had so much work to do?* He thought of the advice and help we would have given to him in the future years. *How can I face the people in our home church if my family has died in the mission field? It can't be possible! How can this be a part of God's plan?* Keith wrestled with God as he tearfully left the terminal building.

Once outside, Keith dropped to his knees on the grassy field next to the parking lot to pray. He looked up into the sky, watching the birds soaring overhead as he prayed out loud. "Lord, You made the birds. I know that You have the ability to keep my family alive no matter how bad the crash. I don't know what happened, but I trust that You will work all things out together for good, just as You promised to those who love You and those who are called according to Your purpose [Romans 8:28]."

As Keith prayed, he had no news as to our condition, but God gave him faith to trust our care to Him, knowing God watches over every situation. He accepted with joy the fact that God never leaves us nor forsakes us. He trusted that nothing could happen to his family apart from His perfect will. The battle was over. He felt peace in his soul.

Opening his eyes, he surveyed the crowd that had gathered to watch this white guy kneeling under the hot sun crying and talking out loud in English. Obviously, they worried about him, so he explained the situation in Swahili. He told them about his Father in heaven who gives hope in time of trial. He took the opportunity to tell them about the blessed hope he had in Jesus. Although he faced the scariest situation of his life and uncertainty about the future, he trusted God with the results.

The compassionate people refused to let him drive his motorcycle after this awful news. So he climbed on the back as another man drove him home. He filled the thirty minute trip with songs, sorrow, and a lot more tears. He arrived at home bracing himself for the worst news he could imagine. Instead, Pastor Mtenzi opened the gate to meet him, shouting, "I just talked to your father. Your family is alive! All of them!"

"All four of them? Thank You, God! I've never been so happy in all my life!"

Soon, Keith made connections with us on the phone to hear firsthand the news of God's miracle. We praised God together.

Chapter 18
PRAISING GOD ON NEWS MEDIA

"Your son's leg is so swollen. Are you sure he's all right?" asked one of the employees in the treasurer's office as we finished a sweet conversation with Keith. In all the excitement, we had failed to notice the swelling on Andrew's leg or the fact that he clung to us unresponsively. Marybeth now realized that Andrew was in shock.

Feeling the leg, Marybeth heard a faint grinding sound. "It's broken," she confirmed. "We need to get it set and put in a cast."

So, after putting a simple splint on the leg, we headed back to the same hospital for treatment. *Bump, bump, bump,* again, as the car slowly jarred its way over the rough lava rocks toward the hospital. Our driver beeped the horn repeatedly at the mob that pressed at the hospital gate. They desperately sought news about loved ones missing since the accident. The armed guards pushed the throng back as our vehicle slowly crept into the busy hospital compound.

An Australian man greeted us in the emergency treatment area. "I just installed the best X-ray equipment in Africa in this hospital a week ago," he proclaimed as we prepared to get an X-ray of the leg. That was news we were glad to hear.

Finally, with X-rays in hand, the attendants led us back into the emergency room. We thanked God they allowed us to offer prayer before the procedure began. We were assigned to Dr. Luci. "It's broken in the upper right femur. We will put the little boy in traction as we put on the cast." As soon as the anesthetic injection had taken effect, the doctor pulled the broken leg gently and then checked to make sure both legs were the same length.

Marybeth held Andrew close as he screamed in fear. "It's OK,

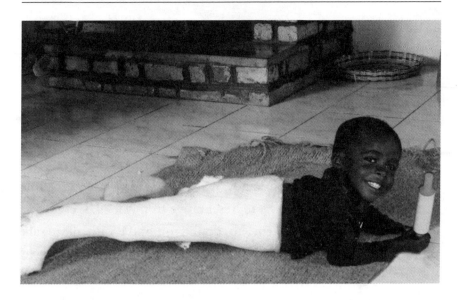

Andrew. The doctor needs to fix your broken leg."

Andrew with his cast after the plane crash.

When had they finished, I could hardly believe what I saw. Andrew now wore a cast from the bottom of his right foot all the way to his rib cage.

"It's called a spica cast," Marybeth explained to me as she saw the look on my face. "They know the procedure and are doing it well."

"Bring him back tomorrow morning for another X-ray," requested Dr. Luci in Swahili. "Then we will see how the ends of the bone look."

We agreed to return the following day.

"Can you tell us how many people died in the crash?" I asked another hospital worker as we left the emergency room.

"We think that more than half of the people

in the airplane died," was the response. "We're treating a badly burned man in the next room, trying to keep him alive, but we don't think he'll make it until morning."

"Oh, Marybeth," I gasped as I felt tears fill my eyes. "Is it really possible that so many died?" I asked in disbelief. This terrible news, the worst news we had heard since the crash, made us sad for our fellow passengers, but even more grateful than ever to be alive.

"Hello. My name is Jim Panos." A voice startled me out of this latest shock. "I am the Goma representative from the U.S. embassy. I am so sorry for your accident. No doubt you find it difficult to talk about the accident, but many from the press would like to talk to you. If you give me permission, I will release your phone number to them."

"I'm glad to meet you, Jim, but I must say that we've had all we can take for today," I answered wearily. "Give me your phone number. I will talk to my wife and give you an answer in the morning after we have a night's sleep."

"OK, Barry. Let me know if we can do anything for you," he replied understandingly.

We felt a big relief to reach Pastor Manyama's home, where we would stay for the next few days. The mental and emotional strain of this day left us exhausted.

That evening we visited by phone with Laura and Jared in America and rejoiced again in God's deliverance. As we recounted to each other the events of the day, we started to fit the story together.

"Then, the hole you made in the side of the plane must have been the same hole we went out, April. But how could you possibly have torn a hole in the side of the plane with your bare hands. It doesn't seem possible!" I said in amazement.

"The man helped me, but we just kept ripping chunks off until it was big enough for me to get through," April replied.

"The only possible explanation is that God sent your angel to help you open that hole and save the lives of many of us. Then, it seems God used other people to enlarge the opening so that we could pass through," Marybeth stated emphatically.

"God is so good." I repeated again. "And you know, after God has saved us in such a miraculous way, it seems selfish to withhold praise for His goodness to us. I think that tomorrow morning we should give our phone number to the press. What do you think, Marybeth?"

"We'll pray about it, but I think God is impressing you to use the opportunity to give Him the glory and praise for His goodness. Yes, it is the right thing to do," Marybeth affirmed.

"Dad," April said hesitantly, "I wonder if God is using this crash to tell us not to move to Kisangani? Maybe we should just go straight home to Kibidula." April asked a fair question. Was this God's way of telling us not to move to DRC? It seemed to be a strange way for Him to communicate to us. Or was this His way of showing us that He could take care of us through anything?

"April, let's wait a while before we decide anything. We need some time to rest and to collect our thoughts," I replied.

That night none of us slept well. Poor Andrew was learning to cope with the huge cast and total helplessness. He was unable even to turn over, and his throbbing leg caused much pain. Throughout the night, April had nightmares in which her parents did not survive. Marybeth and I tossed, still reliving the horrors of the day. From time to time, we touched Andrew's toes to make sure they were warm. I remembered a client whose leg was permanently injured from an overly tight cast.

Ring! Ring! The clock said one o'clock in the morning. *Now, where is that phone?* I asked myself.

"Hello, Barry. We rejoice that you and your family are OK after the plane crash. I want you to know that we are praying for you. This story is on the news everywhere here." On the other end of the line was one of our Dodge Center church members. "Would you be willing to do an interview with a local television station in an hour or so?"

"Yes, I can do that," I answered groggily.

That was the first of seemingly nonstop interviews. We called the U.S. embassy in the morning, authorizing our name and phone number to be released to the press. The phone just kept ringing. I finished one interview and could hardly lay the phone down before it rang again. We prayed that these news reporters would be faithful in praising God's name in their reports.

We couldn't believe how heavy Andrew was in his cast as we carried him from the car back to the X-ray department in the hospital the following morning. The slightest twist caused him pain, so we had to carry him outstretched in front of us. A case of diarrhea made the already difficult toilet functions especially challenging.

"Hello, this is CNN. Your morning interview went so well on the East Coast that we want to do a live nationwide interview in five minutes. Can you hold?" asked the voice on the end of the line.

"Yes," I answered nervously as I sought a quiet place to talk. Surrounded by noise at the hospital, I could hardly hear their questions. I knew my voice trembled as I recounted over the phone the events of the crash. I hoped the battery would hold out; we had replaced it once already. I tried to give the glory to God and to thank those back home who chose to be our prayer partners. As I did interviews behind the hospital, Marybeth and April did live interviews with Associated Press reporters.

Everything seemed so unreal. We consumed much time dealing with such basic chores as washing the blood out of our clothes, borrowing shoes to wear, longing for eyeglasses, getting a razor and toothbrush, and praying that Andrew's leg would heal properly. We had served in relative obscurity in mission service for more than eight years. Now, we felt rather overwhelmed to have people clamoring to talk to us.

The second set of X-rays did not reveal good news. The upper bone was at a thirty-degree angle out of line from meeting the other end of the bone, leaving a large gap between the two splintered ends. How could this heal? We were told that Dr. Luci had left town abruptly. Again we prayed, "God, show us what to do in his absence." One of the American doctors, a pediatrician who happened to be visiting, saw our perplexity and offered his opinion. "In America, we would pin it. I think it will heal as it is, but it's a judgment call. I would refer it back to the main doctor."

As we carried Andrew to the car, a television camera crew followed us, and we did a short interview from inside the car. Marybeth wasn't too excited about the camera since her black eye was quite noticeable and her nose very tender. On our way home, we decided to stop by the accident site with the faint hope that some luggage might be salvageable.

The street of the accident was blocked off on both ends and guarded by armed soldiers. However, they kindly allowed us to drive to the crash site when we explained that we were survivors. We were not prepared for what we saw. "Marybeth, there's nothing left!" I said in amazement.

The charred remains of the pilot's cabin sat like a tombstone marking the graves of those who had died there the day before. The remains of the surrounding market were nothing but ashes. As I gazed upon the remaining wing tips and the tail of the plane, I wondered how we could possibly have survived this crash. Where the body of the plane had been and where we had been seated remained only a pile of ashes. In the center, a few workers still picked through

the debris looking for bodies. My thought of salvaging luggage vanished as I surveyed the sickening scene. Too stunned to even get out of the car, I stared at those ashes, imagining myself among them. *That should be me,* I thought, *except for God's amazing grace.* Later we learned that only six passengers from the plane itself died in the crash, but about forty people from the market had perished. We were speechless on the trip home for lunch as we realized more fully how amazing God's deliverance had really been.

Mrs. Manyama had a nice lunch prepared for us back at their home. "I'm hungry," I told Marybeth as a plate of food was set in front of me. *Ring! Ring!* The telephone called me to another interview. I tried to be patient as I recounted again for the tenth or fifteenth time the events of the crash. After the twenty-minute interview ended, I eagerly looked for my plate again. *Ring! Ring!* Remembering our pledge to praise God every opportunity we had, I set the plate down again and went to a quiet place to answer the questions.

After this same thing happened for the third time, Marybeth said, "Maybe you should shut the phone off. Your food has gotten quite cold over the last hour, and if you don't shut that phone off, you won't get to eat at all!"

"You're right," I replied as I switched the phone off. "I will see if they have charged another battery for the phone. This one needs recharging again." Some of our calls had been from the Division officers, wishing us well and assuring us that we were in their prayers. What an encouragement!

The next important task was to return to town again to look for eyeglasses. Although we failed to find a place that could help us with eyeglasses that afternoon, we considered it a victory to get toothbrushes and a razor. That evening we had an opportunity to check our e-mails. Amazed, we found a barrage of e-mails filled with encouragement, prayers, and well wishes. I responded with a mass e-mail describing the accident and God's marvelous deliverance. One e-mail from Jetro Dias, a young worker at Kibidula, was a special encouragement to us at a time of uncertainty. "Paul was shipwrecked three times. If it's God's will, go on to Kisangani! Don't be discouraged." We could hardly think of boarding another Hewa Bora flight, but the Lord would open the way if it was His will for us to continue.

We were very anxious about whether Andrew's leg needed to be reset. Marybeth's brother Mark, an anesthetist in Arkansas, offered a good suggestion. "If you can send a digital picture of the X-ray, I will show it to an orthopedist here in our hospital, and he can give you a second opinion."

That evening, I thought about the story of the three Hebrews in the fiery furnace. I could really relate to the story now! I knew that heavenly beings were with us in that flaming inferno helping us to reach safety in time. Like those three Hebrews, I felt that we had faced almost certain death, but God intervened miraculously to save us. I remembered how their deliverance had become a testimony to all the leaders of the world who had gathered there on the plain of Dura. Now, we had the privilege of sharing our story of God's deliverance through the news networks. God had turned near disaster into a chance to glorify His name.

We slept much better the second night, and by the following morning, the clamor for interviews was subsiding. We were grateful to find an optician's office in town, where they tested our vision. Although they did not have the exact lenses we needed, we were happy to get something close.

"Dad, you look so funny in those children's frames," laughed April in the early afternoon when we got our new glasses.

"Oh well, at least I can see again. Praise be to God! Again He helped us when I feared we wouldn't be able to get new ones in Goma. Let's see if we can get a safe flight to Kisangani."

The Air Serv personnel were most helpful. Although they had no available seats on their upcoming flight to Kisangani, they offered to charter a small plane for us to reach Kisangani. "We will charge you only eleven hundred dollars, which is the cost of a one-way flight," kindly offered Mr. Sauvage, the office manager.

As I sat in their office, Lori from the U.S. embassy in Kinshasa called to check on our situation. She asked if we had money, and I explained that although I would use most of the remaining thirteen hundred dollars to pay for the plane flight, I still had two hundred dollars left. After paying the money and completing the flight arrangements, we left to try and buy some shoes.

The cell phone rang again. "Hello, this is Air Serv office. If you return right now, we will refund you all the money for your flight."

"But I don't understand," I stuttered as I tried to comprehend this latest blessing.

After receiving a full refund at the Air Serv office, I sought out the manager. "I was willing to pay what you asked, but what made you change your mind and give us a totally free flight?" I queried.

"When I overheard you telling the embassy that you had only two hundred dollars left, I decided to fly you for free," replied Mr. Sauvage, with a big smile on his face.

"Thank you so much. You provided a big blessing for us! God bless you. May we pray right now?" We gratefully offered thanks to God again for His amazing providence.

That afternoon we borrowed a camera and e-mailed a digital picture of the X-rays to Mark in America. We felt confident that the God who did so much for us would surely heal Andrew's leg too. When we got the reply, we rejoiced. The doctors thought that the leg would heal fine and for now we should leave it alone to heal. We had still another reason to thank the Lord.

On Friday morning, I hastily jotted down a list of the things that had been in our luggage and their approximate value in order to submit a claim for our losses to the Hewa Bora office. We had little chance of receiving any remuneration, but at least a claim would be submitted. I thought we should at least receive a refund for the ticket price since we made it only to the end of the runway. At their office, Hewa Bora offered us a free flight to Kisangani, but I declined in favor of a refund. They understood. I was delighted to again meet the Frenchman who helped April to reach the hospital on the day of the crash. We thanked him again for his kindness and rejoiced to see that his friend had also survived the crash.

Then an *Adventist Review* editor phoned, and we gave him an interview. "Are you fully aware of the amount of attention your story has received across the world?" the man asked as we started the interview.

"Not completely," I replied.

"Well, let's just say it is a major news story and has gone everywhere," he responded. There had been very few interviews that day. Fortunately, our story had become old news to the reporters. *People* magazine had called, but we told them to wait until Sunday for their interview.

It didn't take long to pack on Friday for our Sabbath-morning flight. Although we prefer not to travel on Saturday, our next opportunity would have been a week later. A couple of handbags were the extent of our luggage. We had planned to shop for clothes and shoes on Friday, but businesses were closed for a day of mourning for those who died in the crash.

Chapter 19
A REUNION AND A DECISION

Sabbath morning, we had the opportunity to give our testimony to a group of believers before leaving for the airport and our much-delayed trip to Kisangani. The volcano still spewed its ominous clouds of smoke in the background as we drove to the airport.

It felt as if we had returned to the scene of a very bad dream. We all secretly dreaded the moment when we would take off again from this runway. As we pulled up in front of the departure area, I saw a camera team coming our way. "I hope they are coming to talk to someone else," I said.

"I don't think so," replied Marybeth. "They're coming straight for us."

"Hi, my name is Tony. We represent *National Geographic Magazine.* Our goal is to do a documentary on aviation in the Congo. May we interview your family?"

Soon we stood in front of the Air Serv desk, giving our first full-family interview in front of a camera. We realized God had opened another great opportunity to praise His love and care, this time before the *National Geographic* audience. One of the photographers accompanied us on the flight, because they planned a special emphasis on the work of Air Serv. We nicknamed their company "Air Safe" for April's and Andrew's sakes.

Of course, Andrew could not sit in a seat, so they removed a seat and strapped him to the floor like a piece of luggage. Elated to have an American as our pilot, we chatted with him. He told us that DC-9 airplanes were not designed to land in such a short space as the Goma runway.

Since the crash, we often repeated our memorized scriptures. Oh, how we missed our Bibles that had been burned. Was this a premonition of the future when our Bibles would be taken away at the end of time? How we treasured them now that they were gone and no English Bibles were available to us. We resolved to memorize more Scripture verses in the future. Now, we sang Isaiah 41:10 together as we prepared for takeoff.

"Oh, Daddy, I'm afraid, but Jesus will help me," April said as she buckled her seat belt.

Our palms were sweaty, and we closed our eyes as the propellers whirred to full speed. We had barely started down the runway when the little Cessna 206 Caravan was already airborne. Looking down, I was amazed at how short the runway really looked. For a moment, I saw the awful black spot of ashes at the end of the runway, and then the horrible sight disappeared. *Maybe, we'll experience something like this when Jesus comes again—taking us away from the awful misery and horrible memories of sin.*

For two hours, we flew above mountains and jungle on our way to Kisangani. Fortunately, Andrew slept all the way. Finally, we saw the Congo River and knew we were very near our destination. I held Marybeth's hand as we neared the runway and during our smooth landing. Then the steam of the jungle greeted us as we disembarked.

As we entered the airport lounge, we ran to greet Keith and hug him once again. Even some of the airport employees cheered as they remembered Keith's experience of four days before. Now, they could see the whole family together, and they rejoiced with us. What a grand reunion! Just think—reunion in heaven will be even sweeter than this! We paused again to thank the Lord for His goodness and for answered prayers.

The half-hour drive flew by as we chatted happily. Soon we pulled up to the gate of the rented house that served as Congo Frontline Missions' (CFM) headquarters and had another grand reunion with the Mtenzi family.

They told us how the news of the crash had spread like wildfire. All the church members had been anticipating our arrival, and then came the news of the crash. Of course, they all knew the results of airplane crashes in DRC—all passengers die! The Mtenzi family had prepared a feast that day for our arrival. Then, when they received the news of the crash, the celebration turned into a funeral.

When we phoned the day of the crash and Pastor Mtenzi heard our voices on the phone, he couldn't believe it. He spread the news, but other people could hardly believe it either. It was obviously a miracle! One man had been studying the Bible for some time, and when he heard we were alive, he said, "If the God of this church can save its members from airplane crashes, then baptize me. I want to become a member." Another man had become a church member some years before, but continued to doubt the story of Jonah and the whale, saying it was just a fable. After the story came out that we were alive, he said, "I will wait until I see them. If they are really alive, then I know that the story of Jonah in the Bible is true also."

As we recounted the story of the crash, I noticed that Nuru, the Mtenzis' daughter, sat very quietly. After a while, I discovered why. Nuru attended school in Rwanda and had to board a Hewa Bora flight the very next day to Goma on her way to school. The next day, Pastor Mtenzi literally dragged her onto the plane because she was so terrified.

The next day, we had another celebration when the new Land Cruiser that CFM had ordered two months before arrived in Kisangani by cargo plane. Without any roads from the capital to Kisangani, we had the choice of shipment by plane or boat. We had decided on the plane to avoid the seventeen police checks and numerous robberies along the river route.

We moved into the tiny two-bedroom house with Keith and Wezley (a young man from America who had come to help Keith start the project). This would be our home for the next two weeks. Marybeth was brave to try it. The kitchen was slightly bigger than a closet, and the entire family moved into a single bedroom with one window. The oppressive heat made us thankful for fans. Without the fans, Andrew became overheated almost immediately in his large cast. But we were together and alive and praising God. Everything else seemed insignificant.

When I next checked my e-mail, I found another avalanche of well-wishes and prayers from friends, relatives, and people that I did not even know. We really appreciated the words of comfort and kindness. Although we could not leave Andrew alone in his condition, he slowly learned to drag himself around and play with the Mtenzis' two sons. My job, as always, was to get the accounting caught up and balanced.

Kisangani is an amazing city. The mighty Congo River is navigable all the way from Kinshasa near the west coast of Africa to Kisangani by boat. Stanley Falls prevents further boat travel upstream. Large sections of the city are filled with beautiful homes from the past, with arched entryways and attached garages. This was once a gathering point for Europeans. The city, in earlier times, was a modern jewel carved out of the jungle, complete with hydroelectric power and contemporary sewer and water systems. Kisangani boasted every modern convenience while Europeans freely harvested the rich source of diamonds in the nearby rivers.

Unfortunately, this infrastructure was built with forced African labor. Since independence in the early sixties, very few improvements and little maintenance have taken place. Now, many of the homes are deteriorating. Infrastructures such as street lights, electricity, sewer, and water lines groan under the weight of overuse and under-maintenance. Grass grows up in the city and makes it look like an overgrown village in spite of its population of nearly one million. When the invading armies of Rwanda and Uganda battled in Kisangani for the minerals during 2001, the city was devastated. Vehicles were confiscated, and businesses stripped of everything. The city was largely evacuated. Many buildings are still riddled with bullet holes. Although some commerce has returned, Kisangani retains only a shadow of its former glory. The main visitors now are the two thousand United Nation peacekeepers and those foreigners who come to trade diamonds and other natural resources.

In spite of Andrew's cast and Marybeth's contracting a horrible two-day flu and diarrhea, we finally managed to take a break and go to visit the newly acquired mission property located next to the Congo River.

"We have to walk from here," Keith said as we left the Land Cruiser behind. "We have another couple of miles through the jungle before we get to our property."

"It's hard for me to believe we're still in the city limits. There is nothing but jungle," I said as we walked along on the little footpath. Suddenly, I felt something sting my neck. "Ouch, what was that?" I asked as I swept away the little insect from the back of my neck.

"Oh, those are the biting ants that drop from the leaves along the path," Keith chuckled. "Generally, you get only one at a time. They are better than the *siafu* [army ants] that come by the thousands."

By the time we reached the little tributary that flowed into the Congo River, we were sweating profusely from the oppressive heat and humidity. Twenty loose stalks of bamboo sagged toward the water, forming a rudimentary bridge over the thirty-foot span.

"Are you sure this will hold us?" I asked apprehensively as we carefully tiptoed over the bridge. "Don't worry. I saw people carrying huge loads of produce across this bridge the last time I was here," Keith confidently replied.

"What's that moving in the top of that tree?" Marybeth wondered.

"Oh, it's a snake," Keith said as he leaped ahead to see it better. "I don't know what kind it is, but it's long and green. Cool! It's the first one I've seen."

"I wish it would be the last!" Marybeth said as she left the path to give a wide berth between her and the tree holding the fleeing serpent. "The Lord will have to give me strength to live here. On my own, I don't think I can manage."

After a leisurely one-hour walk, we reached the corner of the new two-hundred-fifty-acre property. Bamboo framed the view of the Congo River. "This beauty is worth the walk," I confessed as I admired the shimmering waters flowing by.

"The river is actually much wider than the two hundred yards we see here. That's actually an island over there, and on the other side of that island is the wider part of the river. The people living in those huts have never heard the gospel. I can't wait until we live here. Then, I can cross by canoe and tell them," Keith said enthusiastically.

On the way home, we talked about all the sights we had seen on our walk. Marybeth recounted the six different kinds of edible fruit she had seen along the way. One thing for sure, Keith had found his place to work on this earth.

That evening, Marybeth and I went for our usual evening walk. Since the accident, simple things, such as walking down the road hand in hand with my wife, seemed sweet and special! Thankful to be alive, I enjoyed God's blessings. However, our reception to DRC had been traumatic. Airplane crash. Sickness. Broken leg. Sweltering jungle heat. We had believed the Lord would show us His will about the possibility of moving to Kisangani on this trip. But even

though Marybeth is a brave woman, I wondered whether the challenge would be too much for her to consider.

"Well, Marybeth, what do you think about moving here?" I asked.

"You know, it's as if God is showing us that He can take care of us through anything. If He can save us from airplane crashes, He can protect us through any trial. I think He wants us to move here," was Marybeth's thoughtful reply.

"I feel the same way, honey. God turned the airplane crash from certain death to a chance to praise His name to the whole world. When I searched my name at the Internet café the other evening, I found more than ten thousand listings. Our praise to God for saving our lives has gone everywhere. Surely, 'All things do work together for good to those who love

Our reunited family after the crash. Back row, left to right: *Jared, Laura, Barry, and Keith.* Front row: *Marybeth, Andrew, and April.*

God.' I think He has showed us that if we step out in faith, He will protect and bless us."

"Then, our decision is made," answered Marybeth. "Let's plan to move."

The next day turned into a beautiful climax to our visit as we took a long ride downriver on the forty-foot wooden canoe that Keith had purchased, along with a 40 hp boat motor. Seeing the lovely water lilies along the way and the beautiful greenery along the shores seemed like a vacation for our minds. We contemplated the new faith venture that lay before us, but we were not afraid. The God who calls us to service is well able to perform miracles in the completion of His will.

Chapter 20
CONGO WORK MOVES FORWARD

A cool breeze tousled his hair as Keith Mosier admired the reflection of the moon on the water 730 feet below the Foresthill Bridge that spanned the American River in northern California. It had been a big day! Keith had just graduated from Weimar College in California, where he had trained to become a pastor. Celebrations of the evening over, he came alone to enjoy the awe-inspiring view one last time. Thankful to have reached this milestone in his life, he paused for a few minutes to contemplate his future in Africa. Rather than returning directly to his car, Keith felt impressed to cross to the other side of the bridge. Startled, he saw a man on the walkway ahead of him. What was the man doing here at one o'clock in the morning?

"Are you OK?" Keith asked the man, who was looking out over the deep expanse below.

"My name's Lester and I guess I'm OK for a few more minutes," replied the man with a shrug of his shoulders. "Tonight's my night on this bridge. You want a beer before I jump?" He spoke with a slight slur from alcohol. The story slowly unfolded. After giving away his few possessions, Lester had driven from San Francisco that evening to jump off this bridge. Keith shivered as he remembered an acquaintance of his who had jumped to his death off this same bridge just one year before. When Lester's girlfriend left him, he became convinced that no one in this world cared whether he lived or died.

Now, the life-and-death struggle began. Keith told him about the parents and friends of the young man who had jumped the previous year. He described how they had mourned his loss and wished they could have him back. Keith told Lester how Jesus had died for him and longed to live inside of him day by day.

Finally, about five o'clock, Lester decided to give life another try and left the bridge. Keith was convinced that he would not jump. Driving slowly back to the Weimar campus, he thanked God for leading him to the bridge that night.

Wherever our family went on our furlough that summer after Keith's graduation, people wanted to hear about the airplane crash and how God had miraculously saved our lives. In early August, we shared again at the Adventist Laymen's Services and Industries (ASI) meetings in Florida. Many people related how they had prayed for us as soon as they heard about the accident on the news.

All too soon, we returned to Kibidula to wrap up our work there. Keith returned to DRC, accompanied by Nathan and Carl Rittenour. Nathan had accepted the invitation to be the development director for CFM. His practical knowledge of how to get things done would be invaluable in the building of a new campus. Carl came to tape and produce a video that could help explain the needs and challenges of the Lord's work in DRC.

Soon after their arrival, the three of them flew to Mbandaka, a city four hundred miles upstream from Kinshasa to learn about and film an ADRA project there. The project involved a canoe that serviced the medical needs for a short distance along the river. That day Keith saw the pathetic health needs of the people.

Malaria, typhoid, and sleeping sickness run rampant along the river. Although one out of eight children die at birth, another one out of five more children die before the age of five. Of course, malaria is the number-one killer. Jani, Keith's laundress, rates as a typical example. She lost two of her eight children during birth and three more to malaria. Finally, her husband succumbed to malaria also.

Almost all of the jungle people have graves near their homes from children who succumbed to disease.

As Keith witnessed these pathetic conditions, his heart ached. With virtually no healthcare whatsoever between Mbandaka and Kisangani, he asked himself how many precious people die each day without hearing the gospel. How many more would go to the grave while still living in spiritual darkness?

For us, concluding our work and packing at Kibidula tugged at our hearts after eight years of service. We sadly said Goodbye to many friends. On our last Sabbath in Dar es Salaam, 150 colporteurs honored us with a grand farewell.

Although we arranged each leg of our trip to Kisangani ahead of time, we did not plan on the maintenance delays for the Air Serv flight in Goma. Over the course of ten days, they postponed the flight four times. We finally felt forced to do something we never wanted to do again—board another commercial airline from Goma to Kisangani. Could the Lord be testing us to see if we really could put all our trust in Him?

As we climbed aboard the CAA jet airplane, memories of the crash raced through our minds. Of course, we prayed together before takeoff. And then the moment we dreaded finally came as we started to lumber down the short Goma runway. I tried to be calm for April's sake, but I have to confess that the faster the plane went, the faster my heart raced. Would we never get off the ground? Finally, we felt the aircraft lift into the air. Some time later, we landed uneventfully in Kisangani.

As our team met together again, we reviewed how the Lord had blessed CFM up to that point. In the first evangelism training session, seventy-four laymen had learned how to do church planting. For some, the one-way trip by bicycle to attend the training had taken three weeks. At the conclusion of the training, the students conducted evangelistic meetings as part of their practical training. Fifty-one people chose baptism in the new church plant. The seventeen students hired as church planters in unentered areas had already spawned seventeen new congregations.

By partnering with ASI, DVD players had been distributed and training provided to six hundred laymen in four major cities in DRC. Now, laymen conduct evangelistic meetings in their own homes. Many baptisms resulted from this program.

A new concept, called the one-day church, has recently been developed by Garwin McNeilus to assist in constructing church buildings around the world. Maranatha Volunteers International administers the program that provides steel frames and roofing sheets for a small church structure. Then, new congregations fill in the walls, doors, windows, and floors with materials of their choice. We praise the Lord that the one-day church program has agreed to send us the framing and roof sheets for all the buildings on our campus.

With these new training facilities about to materialize, we plan to offer more training sessions and expand the number of church planters in 2009. Books have arrived, and the first thirteen literature evangelists are trained and selling books. Soon, medical ministries will begin.

Many discouraged people have lost their ambition, self-esteem, and desire to achieve positive results from their own labors. They simply survive day by day, working only when necessary to satisfy their hunger. Their hopes and dreams have disappeared.

We know Jesus wants to lift them up from their degradation and sin and stir their hearts with a new hope in His soon second coming. With God, all things are possible. We pray for miracles. We are grateful to the many people who have visited our Web site at www .congofrontlinemissions.org to see how they might be able to get involved with the work here.

Just before Christmas in 2008, Keith had a booth at Generation

Keith with Tammy, his fiancée.

of Youth Conference in the United States and shared the story of CFM with the thousands gathered there. A number of young people volunteered to help with the work here.

A month later, Carl Rittenour, back home in Minnesota, used his video camera for a top-secret filming assignment. Hiding the camera, he filmed Keith's marriage proposal to his sister Tammy at the Rittenour home. Her surprise and acceptance are all documented on film. We are thrilled! Soon she will come to DRC as Keith's wife to share in the joy of the work here.

Satan does not give up his ground without a fight. Ten days after our arrival in DRC, things looked dark. A rebel army, led by renegade general Laurent Nkunda, marched on Goma, only about three hundred miles away from us. In a panic, foreigners fled the city as the rebel soldiers routed the Congolese army. We wondered what would happen as we packed a few things in case we would need to evacuate quickly. We prayed earnestly, "Lord, You have opened the way up to now. Please let us continue in our work here. Don't let the project fail in its infancy. We trust in Your mighty power." That night, as the rebels stood on the outskirts of the city, completely victorious, they mysteriously called a ceasefire and retreated. That didn't come as a mystery to us! God is all powerful!

Just a few weeks ago, a tremendous thunderstorm drenched the city at night. Lightning flashed and thunder shook the ground. Suddenly, the light and the sound merged into one great blast that shook the house. Marybeth grabbed my arm tightly as we gathered our senses. After a bit, we heard Keith's voice from down the hall. "Is everybody OK?"

The lightning struck his room through the window. He wanted to leap as electricity charged his room, but he could not move. His body felt momentarily paralyzed, and his lips felt numb as the lightning's power surged through the bed. Soon, he could move again and felt for the flashlight next to him on the bed. The battery inside had exploded. Another battery on his table burned the wood underneath it. We thanked the Lord for the faithful work of Keith's guardian angel! Satan cannot harm us as long as the Lord has more work for us to do! Surely, the safest place in the world is the place where God calls us to be.

Today as we walked along the paths of our new jungle property in the Congo, four-year-old Andrew tramped along by our side. With Marybeth's finger clasped in his hand, he gallantly tried to keep up with our pace. I think about the village of Kisada, where Andrew was born. In a good year, one student out of thirty will pass their national exams and go on to secondary school. Students can pass their classes simply by bringing beer to their teachers. Old ladies with red eyes are still murdered occasionally under suspicion of witchcraft.

Without some help at the right time, Andrew could be resting in a little grave next to his mother in Kisada. Now, we are being repaid by his love for us day by day; we cannot imagine life without him. Now, we feel bonded to Africa in a way that cannot be described. Africa is part of our lives and part of our family.

Do you find God's love impossible to fathom? Adopting Andrew helps me understand as I contemplate how Jesus chose to be bonded to us. We cannot describe or understand God's love for us. Throughout all eternity, we will learn more of how He could reach across seemingly insurmountable barriers to make us His children. Somehow we remember in that rescuing of that starving African baby boy how much we need His help to save us as sinners. We can only thank God for an inseparable bond of love that now exists between us as Christ adopted us into His family.

I believe our Jesus will return soon. I encourage you to ask God to tell you what work He has for you to do in the short time we have left on this earth. Are you returning His love as Andrew returns love to us? When we honestly ask Jesus, He always answers. He will make it clear how you can serve Him. Maybe it's where you are, sharing with neighbors and work associates. Maybe it's the DRC jungle. Or perhaps God calls you to somewhere else in the world. Does your labor satisfy your soul? Jesus longs to take you home. Won't you do your part to hasten the return of Jesus our King? He longs to come back to rescue not only you and me from this sin-sick world, but also the people from dark areas who wait for the message of hope. As we see lives transformed here in DRC, we have a satisfaction that will last for eternity. Are you investing *your* labor into something that will last forever?

Pastor Mtenzi
baptizing in the
Congo River.

Pastor Mtenzi in front
of a typical church in
DRC.

Pastor Mtenzi
traveling nearly
impassable roads
in DRC.

Old women carry
huge loads on their
backs in DRC.

Barry with Pastor
Mtenzi next to a
tributary of the
Congo River.

This man walked four days to attend our training session in Kisangani.

Our Land Cruiser stuck in the mud.

If you appreciated this book, your will also want to read these other mission books:

Mayday Over the Arctic!
Dorothy N. Nelson

"Our one and only engine has failed . . . In an unavoidable descent, the aircraft now plunges us a thousand feet per minute toward a frozen world below." This autobiography of an extraordinary mission pilot, nurse, musician, and founder and director of HELP (Health Education Lifestyle Programs) will inspire you to let God expand your horizons for a fuller life of service for Him.
ISBN 10: 0-8163-2291-0

The Lord's Prayer Through Primitive Eyes
Gottfried Oosterwal

It happened one day among the Bora-Bora, a seminomadic Stone Age tribe who roamed the dense tropical forests of the Upper Tor River Basin in West New Guinea. A group of tribesmen came and asked, "*Nana* [friend], teach us to pray."

Oosterwal, who was studying their language and culture, daily meditated with them on the meaning of the Lord's Prayer in order to be able to translate it into their unwritten language. But, how do you translate the kingdom of God for people who have no political structures? Or "our daily bread" for those who eke out an existence in the jungle on roots, grasses, and an occasional fish?
ISBN 10: 0-8163-2307-0

Three ways to order:

1 Local	Adventist Book Center®
2 Call	1-800-765-6955
3 Shop	AdventistBookCenter.com

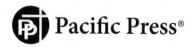 Pacific Press®